THE LOST CROWN OF CUMBRIA

Jonathan Patricks

The Lost Crown of Cumbria

Published by Norman Scotter

ISBN 978-1-904446-33-0

© 2017 Norman Scotter

1st Edition printed 2011
2nd Edition printed 2017

A catalogue record for this book is available from the British Library.

Printed in the UK by
Witley Press Ltd.
24-26 Greevegate, Hunstanton PE36 6AD

www.witleypress.co.uk

Dedication

For Mandy: a sturdy younge lady who came to work on her bicycle – yet never lived to read this edition!

The Celtic Year

Much of The Lost Crown of Cumbria takes place during the festival of Samhain.

The main purpose of Celtic Festivals was to ensure a good harvest; therefore they happened at the times of the year that were important to farmers. Folk gathered together from outlying farms at the Tribe's Holy place and there was much feasting and merrymaking. Above all, these occasions were religious and sacrifices were made to the Gods to encourage fertility.

IMBOLOC (1st February). The festival took place at lambing time and was to celebrate the ewes were producing milk. Samples of sheep milk were often offered to the Gods in special places – often under oak trees which were sacred.

BELTAINE (1st May). The name of this festival means Bel's Fire or Goodly Fire. At Beltaine the Celts lit fires topped by poles symbolising the Sacred Oak Tree. Cattle were driven through the flames to purify them and protect them from disease. Druids often made sacrifices and prayed to their Gods for a fruitful year.

LUGHNASA (1st August). This was the festival or feast of Lug. At this time, folk put on a play and all the Tribe watched – about feeding the Tribe and protecting it from others.

SAMHAIN (1st November). Samhain – the end of Summer was the most important festival of all – and the beginning of the New Year – to encourage the land to prosper and to celebrate the marriage of the Tribal God to a Nature Goddess. The eve of Samhain (the Celtic day began on the eve of the following day) and was a magical time when strange events happened.

Prologue

It was in AD 945 when rank upon rank - the Saxon Shield Wall of Edmund the Saxon King moved upwards like a gathering storm. Onwards they came, step by step, with the clashing of sword upon sword - onwards, ever onwards - towards the top of the pass! Awaiting them rank upon rank - silent and determined - shoulder to shoulder - the steel shod folk: of the mountains with their King, their Lord and Master - guarding the gateway to an ancient Celtic Kingdom.

"DUNMAIL

Scene of Battle
Mount of Stones - Grasmere, Keswick Road

The walls of shields met head on - and many a brave roan sank within the following melee. Back and forth swung the battle ordered men. This way! That way - stormed the lines of steel midst the blare of the Carnyx - the Celtic war trumpet!

"OWT! OWT! OWT! OWT! OWT! OWT! "

- bellowed the Saxon House Curls. Down crashed ^{then-}battle axes! Time and lane again the onslaught was halted! Backwards and forwards went the crush of the battling warriors. But little by little the lines began to thin - and had it not been for Malcolm of Scotland fighting with King Edmund - then Dunmail would have had the day.

In the end some say Dunmail lay dead and the Celtic nation were done forever! But 'twas said King Dunmail's golden crown was rescued and thrown into a turn on high. Beneath the waters it settled - and because of the crowns magical properties it would renew the claim to lands - then lost - to be ever disputed!

THE GEORGE HOTEL

ONE

The Gathering Storm

The skies over Beacon Edge were cloudy and a stormy day was approaching. It was a Sunday morning and the rain lashed people of the parish were making their way to Saint Botolph's Church. A special morning service was to take place - one to celebrate the three hundredth anniversary of the installation of The Five Saints. The Bishop of Carlisle would be there to take part in Holy, Communion therefore the occasion at Saint Botolph's was well attended.

When the Bishop entered to make the processional entrance the organ began to play and everyone began to sing the first. hymn. Soon after came the sermon and the prayers. Shortly the Sacrament of Holy Communion began!

But at this point in time - a hullabaloo erupted at the rear of the congregation. People gaped and stared in astonishment when several short people with wild staring eyes ran down the aisle and snatched the Gold Goblets standing upon the Altar Then in an instant the wide-eyed creatures ran back and out of the Church. At, first the congregation was too shocked to make a protest -- but then the indignant cries began.

"Send .for the police!" bellowed one particular person.

"This is disgraceful!" cried another:

"This should never be allowed!" thundered the crowd.

No sooner had the Boggarts ran out of the Church and down the lane towards the town centre - the Church Warden appeared in a most distressed state of mind wringing his hands in despair!

"They've also stolen the Bishop's solid gold candlesticks!" he shouted

Horror of horrors - the church emptied almost at once when the whole congregation ran out in hot pursuit of the Brood of Boggarts. Down the lane they chased them towards the town's main road and beyond along the way leading to Beacon Edge's ruined medieval castle

This was far from the end of the matter! The angry crowd - shouting and protesting - were just about to lay their hands on the scoundrels when - in a frenzy to escape capture - the Boggarts scrambled to the top of the highest pile of the castle's sandstone remnants. There they turned and one by one - holding the gold goblets in their plate-like hands - jumped into space and:

VANISHED!

On the other hand Joe the Tramp happened to be staying at The George Hotel in Beacon Edge. Many folk in the small country town knew him by sight where his sharp blue eyes commanded attention. As did his sharp nosed, features and his long grey hair reaching down to his shoulders. His long flowing white beard ended at the belt of an old gabardine coat but the most striking thing about the Tramp were his shiny black shoes that never seemed to get dirty.

And there he sat indulging in polite conversation over breakfast about the headlines in the national press:

THE QUEST FOR GOLD!

"Have journalists at last discovered its value?" asked a certain old lady - card set the tables on a roar!

"If the Chinese hear of this they'll be here to buy up the whole county!" remarked someone from the corner of the room.

The Tramp at first joined in the laughter- but at the back of his mind there was the realisation the problem was only beginning. It was said the Chinese were short of all kinds of metals and would buy up whole mountains to feed their development as a nation!

"So what would happen if anyone assumed Cumbria had much gold?" thought the Tramp. "It would need a hero to save this land - and who would that be?"

At that moment the under manager entered the room and whispered to one of the waitresses who was a resident of the town. The occasion caught the eagle eye of the Tramp who smiled at the young lady and politely asked for her attention.

"Well sir;" replied the young lady "Our Five Saints sir -the ones in Saint Botolph's Church - I've just been told one of them has turned their back on us! My dad tells me this could mean something really bad is going to happen here in Beacon Edge!"

Joe the Tramp somehow had expected this - it was now known throughout Cumbria the misfortune of the Golden Goblets having been stolen.

The Tramp merely smiled at the news and allowed the young waitress to carry on with her duties - but inwardly he was most concerned and his usually happy expression turned to one of anger - and furthermore one of fear of approaching troubles.

The young waitress left the breakfast room and many guests got to their feet and began to make for the hotel's entrance hall - when the tables around them and the crockery and other table wear began wobble and tinkle. The chandelier in the ceiling began to sway and rumblings came from the ground below!

"The first saint has turned!" mumbled the Tramp in horror and sat down in the hotel lounge when the rumbles subsided and then -

STOPPED!

The Tramp decided he must seek out several rumours - the ones most likely to the source of coming misfortune! Golden coloured vans had been reported around the sleepy village - and in the afternoon Joe the Tramp headed north with Napoleon and the Big Green Caravan.

Saint Botolph's Church in Beacon Edge was famous for its row of five saintly stone statues. These were known locally as The Five Saints. These were the first call on any guide's list for visiting tourists. The Five Stone Saints were to be found in a previous church long before Saint Botolph's was built - and was said to have been endowed with great magical powers of healing - where before the Middle Ages many folk journeyed to be cured of various illnesses. But there was a legendary tale that should any profound evil happen to the locality - the Saints - one by one would turn their backs on the world. Should the last Saint turn in disgust - it was said - the church would crumble to dust making it impossible for the powers of evil to enter it and claiming it for their own.

*****

A little: further south from Beacon Edge - Barny was looking out of the window at the busy street below. It was a hot bustling morning in Ambleside where streams of shoppers of all kinds were passing by - hikers, tourists, streams of children escorted by harassed teachers. One of these caught his eye. A tall lanky fellow holding his top hat in his hand escorting a line of curious children odd looking children, but children dressed as others were dressed. At first Barny felt a little confused but when he looked again at the tall lanky chap holding a drooping very tall top hat - deep within his mind a bell rang!

HIGH HAT!

"Walter!" shouted Barny, "come here and look at what I can see!"

But by the time Walter had come through, from the rear of the flat where they were staying - High Hat and the small people he was leading had merged within the crowds

"You're being obsessed Barny - you appear to spot him everywhere."

"Well what about it? High Hat could be anywhere - even here in glorious Ambleside.

Barny was about to let the matter drop - they argued endlessly upon this particular point of view but on this occasion he persisted with his own opinion.

"Just imagine we. found him and discover what the crooks are up to?"

"OK you win!" growled Walter; "- but don't blame me if it's just a waste of time!"

They left their lodgings and followed the direction High Hat had been walking. But dodging through the mass of tourists crowding the pavements was quite exhausting. Searching the crowded shops and restaurants was quite out of the question therefore they decided to find a seal and chance upon seeing the Prince of All Evil.

"You do realise we're on a fool's errand?"

"Do you Walter-" replied Barny"- well do you see what I can see."

Across the road was a store catering for walkers and clinchers. There -just beyond than an angry shop assistant holding a pair of protesting children by the ears!

"Shop lifters!"- smattered Walter;

"Some thieves - they may be!" chuckled Barny "If you think they're normal children then think again my friend - they 're Boggarts!"

The pavement outside the shop became blocked when more so-called 'children' ran out of the store each holding a large golden flag in their hand At first they merely protested. But soon the dwarf-like creatures began to kick and scream. Eventually more little people emerged from the shop. Very quickly a melee of angry tourists and dozens of small people were gathered on the pavement.

"Where is High Hat?" asked Walter:

"Don't worry about High Hat ?" replied Barny, "he'll be somewhere around!"

EEOR! EEOR! EEOR! EEOR!

A distant police siren was heard and the furore on the far pavement became even more ferocious but when the wailing drew nearer the situation altered and various stolen items were quickly thrown aside by the dwarf-like scoundrels who shot away in every direction.

"Now what more proof do we need," asked Barny "- of High Hat being up to his villainous tricks again?"

Two policemen appeared and began to question the crowds of bystanders - but the two young men had seen all they needed to see and realised the Devil himself had returned!

Days later they left Ambleside far behind them - including Mrs Cobbly's Bed and Breakfast business in her double fronted house on the town's main thoroughfare and began the climb to Kirkstone Pass.

In due course they were halfway along the narrow country road the locals called 'The Struggle' - a steep and narrow country road leading to the Pass - the gap in the mountains leading to Ulfswater

But the famous Kirkstone boulder lodged deeply at the top of the Pass was a long way ahead. Eventually they stopped by the wayside to admire the view and there behind them - towards the horizon - lay the long shining waters of Grasmere.

"What a tranquil scene!" murmured Barmy!

"Gad!" quipped Walter; " - to think we were penned up among the hustle and bustle of Uni!"

It was too early for most drivers to launch themselves into the heat of a promising summer's day - but there was ever the prospect of a nutty coach driver trying to decant his wide high-sided vehicle along the 'Struggles' narrow undulating road

Barmy Smithson and Walter Brighton had graduated at university - and were nearing the end of a walking holiday. And what was more - they were hoping to find a job in the coming autumn. Now they were taking a breather before they hopefully entered the world of work.

The sun glared down and two walkers began to perspire. Presently they'd succeeded in reaching the top of the rise and below the hat sun they rested on the grassy verge. They opened their rucksacks and began to enjoy the packed lunches prepared by Mrs Cobbly.

CAW! CAW! CAW!

The two young men looked upwards to where a lone telegraph pole stood beside them - whereupon sat -

THREE BLACK CROWS!

"Oh! Surely not them again!" - ex-claimed Walter.

This was no idle comment - not long ago Big Black Crows were an evil omen possibly Boggarts who 'd change their form. One of them perched up high - gave a knowing blink towards them and opened its beak as if to sneer: Then - in flash - they spread their wings and flapping loudly headed for- the top of the rise ahead of them.

Later having had their fill - namely meat pies - beef sandwiches and bottles of Ginger Beer - the shouldered their rucksacks and once again began trudging along the steep rise ahead.

RUMBLE! RUMBLE! RUMBLE!

The sound of approaching traffic drew their attention. A line of motorists slowly passed them. Finally an oversized van -.an unusually coloured van - a van painted in gleaming gold - raced towards them.

"What the heck?" shouted Barny shielding eyes from the glare.

"Watch out!" bellowed Walter, "there's a. fool corning at us!"

Careering, from one side of the road to the other- the golden van rushed towards them. Barny and Walter had to leap for their lives-

WHAM!

"Gad!" yelled Walter shaking his fist,"- what a stupid fool!" They picked themselves up from the long grasses – and Barny repeated the slogans he'd seen on the vans -

TIP TOP INVESTMENTS

"Look out Barny here comes another one!"
Once again they had to jump clear!

WHAM.'

They heard a blaring of a horn!
"And another one yelled Walter!"

WHAM.'

Once again they had to jump clear!
"Blast you!" shouted Walter at the sight of the speeding vehicles.
"Exactly" retorted Barny. "Peace and quietness of the Lakes? At this rate no one will ever come here!"
They went on in silence. But it wasn't until they'd topped the last rise and entered the Inn at the top of the Pass that a sense of normality surrounded them. There was no trace of High Hat here and the two graduates began planning the next stages of their journey.
First of all," said Walter;"- I'm having one of Pete Pepperson's special ice creams!"
Peter Pepperson was a well-known and exceedingly revered old gentleman who owned a general store in Glenridding - an establishment selling everything a tourist would require - and because of this he had

become a very wealthy inhabitant of the valley. Furthermore his knowledgeable history of the area outstripped the information one would find in the wealth of guide books residing in his store.

On leaving the Inn it took over two hours of determined plodding down Kirkstone Pass before the village of Glenridding came in sight and a further hour before they entered it.

"Forget the ice creams!" said Walter "What about having a pint of beer over there!" and pointed towards the hotel in question - but a second glance stunned them! In the Glenridding Hotel's car park stood one of the big shiny golden vans they'd seen before advertising:

TIP TOP INVESMENTS

Walter grabbed Barny by the arm saying:

"Come on - we must suss this one!" and they hurried across to the entrance of The Glenridding Hotel.

Once they entered the hotel's lounge they were impressed by its feelings of comfort - the shiny appearance of the bar and its impressive rows of coloured bottles and glasses - and the well-dressed uniformed waiters.

"Barry!" said Walter nodding his head towards the bar "He looks familiar!"

An older person had caught his eye - a smallish, rounded, pot-bellied person - a jovial character with a large protruding Roman nose - standing with one arm propped on the bar.

But Barry was quite unimpressed and had noticed the brooding clouds over distant Pooley Bridge!

"Well Walter," he said. "We'd best be away to find the place before the showers begin!"

Having promised to keep a long standing appointment with Joe the Tramp they realised they would have to hurry. But the storm noticed by Barny now appeared as a boiling cliff of cloud surging upwards to the very heights above them - and then - down came the rain!

They half ran, half walked through the downpour hoping to see Joe somewhere ahead. But this never occurred and after many miles of miserable wet walking by Ulfswater they eventually crossed the stone bridge over the River Eamont and entered the busy village of Pooley Bridge (locally known as Poolah!) - where through the rattling rain they observed a long line of parked vans - all painted in shiny brilliant gold bearing the slogan Tip Top Investments!

"Gad!" gasped Barny, "why should anyone need so many vehicles? "

"Because business is apparently booming!" replied Walter "Whatever that is!" replied Barny.

But the downpour increased and the gale began to blow increasingly hostile. They decided to stay the night but after making endless enquiries the whole village had no lodgings available. Of course it was a high point in the tourist Season and it was to be expected.

"What about the bridge," chuckled Waiter; "We could shelter there and bivouac, under it and keep the waterfowl company - at least we'll be sheltered from any showers of rain? "

They made themselves comfortable by the side of the lapping waters as best as they were able. It became dark and the rain stopped and the moon broke through the clouds and hovered high overhead They slumbered a little but around three o'clock in the morning they heard the sound of vehicles starting, doors slamming and the incessant chatter of voices.

"Now what?" asked Barny.

"Search me!" replied Walter

Later they heard the rumblings of vehicles driving away.

Then - within a minute or two they dozed off to sleep again. The dawn came and went- and they began the walk to Beacon Edge. Where not too far ahead they came across a side road where they discovered oily skid marks blackening the road

"Come on Barny!" said Walter pointing a hand" - let's follow this road sign - think about those golden vans - we may discover what they're up to!"

But Barny hesitated- sensing the road ahead was more than what it seemed to be! The sun was shining but the feeling of apprehension was somehow still within them!

*****

But at that very moment in tune way down the map at the southern tip of Ulfswater stood -

HARTSOP HALL

This was a well-known historic dwelling. But at this time within this abode certain strange events were

occurring where a lady endowed with mysterious abilities was laughing.

It was not a normal laugh but a crafty scheming laugh - the laugh of a crafty ingenious -

ENCHANTRESS!

It was dark but she could see as she pleased if not through her eyes - but in other devious ways. She was clever, she was wise and she was well aware of it. There were mysteries about her and what was more she sensed the presence of someone else in the locality - a person who was as clever and as well versed in the ways of the world of magic as she was.

The room about her was dark and she ambled from one side of it towards the spiralled staircase that led below to her special place - a room where her spell-making - and other incantations were performed. Mad Eliza they called her - but mad she may be - most living souls gave her a wide berth and those living nearby whispered about evil spirits being her guardians.

Eliza took up her broomstick and went over to where an iron staircase led below - down, down, she stepped to the cellar: There she approached a trapdoor in the cold living rock. The Enchantress listened to the rushing chorus of a hastening stream and the comings and goings of - echoes of subterranean winds - whirling through the passages around her There before her in the floor was the iron encrusted trapdoor that creaked and groaned when she pulled it back.

Once it was let down behind her she stepped over to the far wall of a large chamber - where upon a wall there hung a huge golden mirror; Eliza then reached out to where her black pointed hat stood upon a shelf - placed it upon her head and began to mutter,

"MIRRROR,.MIRROR UPON THE WALL -
WHO IS THE WORST ONE OF THEM ALL?

At first the Golden Mirror became frosted and two black lines appeared. These quickly became two staring eyes. A long nose appeared followed by a wide sneering mouth - then - and only then -did a very high top hat appear!

HIGH HAT!

"Now let all the powers that be - quickly! quickly! - harken to me!"

Eliza the Enchantress stretched her hand forward and put her hand through the mirror and grabbed the smoke-stack hat.

VOILA

And was High Hat surprised? The mirror frosted! The angry face -

VANISHED!

"But where be you Prince of All Evil?"
Eliza the Enchantress turned and walked to the back of the cavern to thrust the Hat into the depths of a simmering cauldron. There she stirred the bright liquid - and from a shelf high on the wall Eliza seized - one by one - several brightly coloured concoctions and poured them into the steaming cauldron.

Mad Eliza threw back her head and laughed shouting a well-known spell:

"LOLLIPOP! POLLI-POP! DOLLI-POP!"

She stood back and waved her wand! Presently a twisted shape came out of the simmering broth and rose upwards - ever so slowly - and began to assume the, form of a small oak tree. From the leaves of the oak tree - coloured vapours come into view and began to write a message in the air!

The eyes of the Enchantress gleamed when she read it and slowly turned to yet another shelf - where many volumes of magic stood waiting.

"So that's the place!" said she. "Then my hounds will lead me to it! Therefore it is an oriental spell I need!"

Slowly and deliberately she thumbed through the pages - and suddenly exclaimed:

"Here is one that will do the trick!" and from what was writ began to speak!

"OMNIVAR! OMNIVAR! THUS DO GO ABOUT!
"THRICE TO THINE! AND THRICE TO MINE!
AND THRICE AGAIN TO MAKE IT NINE!
PEACE! THE CHARM 'S WOUND UP "

'And row to see my petty ones," said Eliza lowering her wand.

She turned towards the cauldron and after retrieving High Hat's tall topper from the broth - Eliza made her way to the rear of the Great Hall - with the coloured vapours looping ahead of her: Presently there came a chorus of baying hounds. Out in the cobbled farmyard at the rear of the Hall - Eliza was greeted by them who leapt and bounded towards her.

"There, there my precious one," said Eliza who stroked and patted them allowing them to sniff the scent on High flats topper:

How they yowled with delight and began roaming ahead of her: Finally they left the yard and went out into the dawning's light. Far beyond them all - went the looping twinkling vapours - through the woods and open meadows.

On they went at an amazing speed - as if they merely hovered above the ground. After proceeding over vast distances in a short space of time - they reached the top of a hill. There the Enchantress looked down upon a stately home surrounded by vast acres of parkland. All this she saw when all about there came a great silence where -

NO BIRD MOVED OR SANG!

"So my adversary lives over yonder?" A most able individual they must be - to be my equal in the art of magic!"

TWO

The Inn Of 'The Red Boar'

Barny and Walter had walked many miles underneath the blistering heat of the sun. After leaving Ambleside they had reached Askham a country village north of Ulfswater

"Look here!" said Barny, pointing to a line of scorched tyre marks, "would you agree whoever made these must have been driving at speed! But why in a sleepy little place like this?"

Barny and Walter looked about them at the cherished lawns and white-washed houses – their owner's cars shining clean and parked discretely – but Barny was still suspicious!

"I don't like the vibes around here,' he whispered. 'And I sense trouble!'

They were about to plod onwards when they observed an attractive Inn on the far side of the wide village green – a quaint little place built in a mock Tudor style with an ancient sign swinging from its timbers

"The Inn of the Red Boar!" cried Barny, "It sounds interesting," – a wide grin spreading over his face.

"Notice the stone arched entrance leading to a yard at the back," said Barny, "– obviously in the past it must have once been an old coaching Inn."

CAW! CAW! CAW!

The two friends glanced upwards and there staring down upon them from a telegraph pole they saw –

THREE BLACK CROWS!

"Not those again!" bellowed Walter.

"CAW! CAW!" CAW!"

"Go on!" shouted Barny – "Shoo!" – and away flew the three black crows.

They crossed a wide stretch of lawn, approached the Inn's open door and walked into the lounge to find themselves quite alone. They pressed the buzzer upon the bar and waited. No answer! Walter pressed the buzzer once again.

NO REPLY!

Presently a stream of thirty customers entered and congregated in front of the bar. Once again the buzzer buzzed and the newcomers shouted something quite inaudible. Someone entered from the back and host of friendly chattering began.

"Walter!" whispered Barny, who'd caught a glimpse of someone, "– look who's serving behind the bar!"

Chatting contentedly to his customers was a person they'd noticed in The Glenridding Hotel – a smallish, rounded, pot-bellied person with a large Roman nose.

"I wonder! Do you reckon he's the Landlord?" said Barny,

Walter grimaced and said nothing.

Minutes later, after turning things over in his mind, Barny whispered:

"Walter – it's only a hunch – let's have a look at the yard at the back."

Without waiting to be served, they made their way by the gossiping group of drinkers towards the exit at the rear of the room.

"Just as I thought!" growled Barny.

There before them were parked three shiny golden vans, bearing the sign – Tip Top Investments!

Tentatively, they crossed the cobbled yard and in turn – ever so quietly – opened the doors of the three vans.

"Completely empty!" groaned Walter.

"Of course they are – the first thing they'd do would be to shift the stuff!"

Peals of laughter were heard from within the Inn followed by the sounds of approaching footsteps.

"Someone's coming into the yard!" said Barny.

"Come on! Climb those stairs!" urged Walter looking to where a short flight of steps ended at a loft-like room on the first floor of a farm building.

The clatter of footsteps came nearer.

Within the room they remained silent – and listened – and overheard something that had been discussed at the bar – something important and of major concern.

"OK Wilf – now what do we do?" said someone.

"Nothing! We'll wait for orders from the top!" replied another.

"His Nibs' you mean?" said the first speaker.

"For Pete's sake don't call him that!" replied the second.

The footsteps retreated and the yard quietened! A door opened within the Inn and the voices from within the bar grew louder – the door closed!

SILENCE!

Barny and Walter looked about them. The room was what one would expect within an old country building – a straw covered floor, farm tools – pitchforks and other farming implements hung from the walls – horse's harness, old coats and soil riddles.

"There's nothing here Walter – let's go further in and explore!"

They investigated further and the daylight began to dim, making them blunder into obstructions.

Voices were heard from the yard.

"Jack, did you hear that?"

"It might be the cat?"

"Not on your life! There's somebody up there!"

"Come on then! Let's find out!"

Whoever they were began to climb the wooden steps.

Barny and Walter looked about them – peering into the darkness. Only to find the only way out – was by way of another flight of stairs.

"Come on Barny, let's see what's above us."

They tiptoed upwards and stepped into a room quite similar to the one below – bleak stone walls – masses of cobwebs and a floor covered in straw.

"They may be up 'ere in the top room!" they heard someone say.

"Aye! Well go on up then!" replied another.

TREAD! THUMP! TREAD!

The two friends froze – overwhelmed by fear.

"Do something; they're nearly at the top of the steps!"

"Look! Here's an opening in the wall!" exclaimed Walter, "– come on look smart!"

Barny didn't even look and seeing the gap in the wall jumped into it!

They went – one after the other – to find them pitched among layers of straw scattered upon the floor of a wooden farm cart.

"Whatever was that we shot down?"

"A grain-shoot Walter – and we'd better lie low for a while – you never know who's around!"

And there they remained quite composed, until they heard the clatter of steel shod soles upon the cobbled yard below, followed by more voices –

"The place was empty! I even searched the room at the top!"

"Whoever they were – they'll be miles away by now!"

Within the straw-bedded cart, Barny was suddenly about to sneeze. Walter grabbed him and pushed his head among the straw.

Once again there came voices from below.

"We'd better get in touch with 'his nibs' again – if he finds out about this we'll be for it!"

THE CLATTER OF IRON SHOD SOLES!

– echoed around the yard and quickly diminished, and the two young men were left alone.

"Did you hear the bloke say – we'd be miles away?"

"Fat chance that would be!" replied Barny. "So how do we do it?"

"Those golden vans parked in the yard?" replied Walter. "We are in a very tricky position here! Say we escape by borrowing one and driving away?

But quite unknown to the two friends – somewhere in Askham village, Joe the Tramp sat in the darkness – his only grasp on reality was when the shuffling of feet went by the door – and the grumblings of unknown people – when passing.

Joe the Tramp had been captured after making enquiries. Enquiries about certain rumours spreading around Ulfswater – and here he was reflecting upon them. Joe had been imprisoned for less than a day, and he was hungry and thirsty. Being completely at the mercy of his captors, Joe was more than concerned. He knew he had stumbled upon something important – and knowing his adversaries had much to lose. So here he sat and waited and waited.

CREAK!

His cell door opened and he was hauled to his feet by two shady looking characters and hustled along a passage and into the light of day.

"Now old man, you're going to see 'his nibs'," explained one, "– so if you're wise you'll co-operate – or else another spell in the sin-bin!"

"Come with us," – ordered another who grabbed Joe by an arm – and marched him towards the open door of a lift. Once inside they zoomed upwards. When the elevator's door flew open the Tramp was hustled onwards – this time into a darkened room!

"Be seated!" – ordered someone beyond and a square piece of cloth was placed over his face.

The Tramp became aware of a bright light shining upon him – and then without warning – the cloth was removed. When Joe opened his eyes he looked into the blinding light of an array of powerful lamps. Yet behind the bright lights, Joe was just able to discern the head and shoulders of a dark figure – then a distorted voice spoke to him through a special microphone –

"Why are you meddling in my affairs?"

"Meddling?" snapped Joe.

"You heard what I said Mr Joseph – therefore don't you dare speak to me like that!"

Not a further word was uttered!

"Alter your ways my friend – do not dabble in other people's affairs and all will be well. You are free to go this time – but should I lay hands upon you again – or upon others who support you – expect the worst!"

The voice hiding behind the blazing light remained silent – until it said slowly –

"What do you know about The Time of the Ancients?"

Joe had heard of the term before, but not knowing the complete answer, he held his peace. His silence was rewarded by being propelled towards another room and told to sit down and wait.

The Tramp waited for a whole hour then the door before him –

CLICKED!

– then swung open. Joe got to his feet and walked towards the open door.

There before him was open parkland filled with magnificent trees and the sounds of clean running water and there only a few yards away Napoleon was ready and waiting between the shafts of the Green Caravan. The Tramp walked forward and climbed aboard the reining seat and Napoleon ambled away turning his back upon a large stately home.

Joe turned – and there standing behind him in the back of the Green Caravan was a large golden coloured bitch called Dusty. But the Tramp was keen to get moving and with a jerk of the reins Napoleon began to trot.

On the other hand – not very far away – Eliza the Enchantress – had also been making enquiries. These were subtle investigations that only an Enchantress could accomplish in the few hours since her arrival.

Eliza was well aware of what would have happened within the stately home.

Now she had arrived at the spot – where down below stood the stately home her hounds had scented – the spot where High Hat had his headquarters.

A Green Caravan was heading towards her – upwards along the winding track to where she was standing. Not far behind there followed a large golden van.

Eliza stood tall – poised with a wand in her hand. The Green Caravan when at the top of the rise, pulled off the road and came to a standstill. The shiny Golden Van came up behind and from within the van two young men leaped out and joined Joe the Tramp and the Golden Retriever on the reining seat.

Eliza smiled – in appreciation of the smart manoeuvring – but the smile vanished when she heard – the loud blare of a horn!

– a signal to the Boggart Brood hiding within the grounds of Askham Hall. Now the wide-eyed dwarfs were coming out of the gateway of the Hall and onto the village street, bellowing in anger and crowds of them began racing up the hill towards the Green Caravan.

Eliza waved her wand and shouted:

"BE STILL FOOLS OF THE FELLS!"

The entire Brood below stopped dead in their tracks!

The Enchantress turning towards those in the Green Caravan saying

"Joseph where are you going?"

"To Beacon Edge Madam!" replied the Tramp.

The Enchantress looked very serious and replied, "Depart Joe the Tramp and remember High Hat's magic is coming to the flood!"

The journey to Beacon Edge was accomplished before lunch time and who should be trotting behind the Tramp? When they walked into the town, everything gave the impression things were normal. People were on the streets going about their business and all – as they assumed – was well with their world!

THREE

The Mystery Of Grisedale Tarn!

High above the village of Glenridding the nearby fells dominated the scene. But on the slopes of a low ridge overlooking the village – within a rambling old and mysterious house – two men were in earnest conversation. One of these was Joe the Tramp and the other a well-known personality Peter Pepperson. They were discussing what had been discussed over breakfast at The George Hotel regarding the search for gold and other rumours spreading around the area.

CRACKLE! CRACKLE! CRACKLE!

A log fire was burning brightly and the household's Ginger Tom was spread-eagled upon the carpet before it and nearby but well beyond in the corner of the room lay Joe's new friend – a Golden Retriever.

"Now the thing that bothers folks hereabouts," remarked Peter Pepperson, "– if the rumours are correct about finding gold here and the scarring of these hills by prospectors comes true – then tourists would stop coming. Should this happen incomes here would drop!"

"And therefore friend Peter?"

"Find who's behind all this!" he replied. "To say gold is to be found round here in Ulfswater is a bit farfetched

– and if it is – then it should be simple to find the folks who say so!"

At that moment his elderly wife Sarah entered holding a tray of tea and cakes – the white iced ones with a red cherry on the top!"

"If you ask folk round here," announced Sarah, "– they'll say there's too many strange goings on hereabouts. Funny things happen – if someone's on the make around this spot – they've got uncanny powers! Magic may be! Things hereabouts that can't happen – do happen!"

"But it is also said that the spirit of a dead King roams this part of the world," chuckled the Tramp. "Could this be true?"

"Aye! Dunmail you mean?" said Sarah.

"Don't attract fate my lass," replied Peter. "There's many a true word said in jest!"

"The story goes – I'm told," the Tramp replied:

"DUNMAIL THE LAST KING OF CUMBRIA!

– lost a battle on the raise above Grasmere?"

"Aye that's true Joe," replied Peter, "and furthermore his crown was thrown into Grisedale Tarn – a King's Crown with magical properties!"

"Like an Arthurian Legend?" replied the Tramp? "To right all wrongs – and put things to rights?"

"Aye that's right Joe – but it's going to take more than that if there are prospectors snooping around here!"

The room went silent – but Joe recovered to say:

"Prospectors? Around here in glorious Ulfswater? Surely not!"

31

"Aye Joe – that's right!" replied Sarah. "If they are around here and start their digging – there goes wonderful Patterdale!"

"And Glenridding my lass!" grumbled Peter and gazed into the brightness of the fire – reflecting upon the shiny horse-brasses pinned upon the gnarled timbers across the room. The Tomcat before the fire snored and only the laughing fire broke the silence.

"What a sorry prospect Peter!" replied the Tramp. "But that will need – Financial backing?"

The cat snored louder.

"And even more – whoever they are," the Tramp continued, "– surely they will have to be granted official permission to carry out mining?"

"Come on Joe!" laughed Sarah, "Where have you been all your life! You know what they say in certain places – a nod's as good as a wink!"

Sarah laughed raucously and continued arranging the tea and cakes.

It was a thoughtful man who made his way down the hill to Glenridding who looked back to wave goodbye to Peter and Sarah. Joe turned and once again stepped slowly down the hill to where the Green Caravan was parked in a nearby meadow.

That evening Joe ate his supper slowly and when he decided to turn in for the night slept very little dreading what may come to pass! But Dusty his amiable friend sat quite aware that Joe was dreaming

As the Tramp slumbered – his imagination ran riot – where endless chains of high level gantries carried tubs full of spoil on lines of thick wire hawsers – dominating whole ridges of the fells around Ulfswater. Joe's relentless imagery went out of control and there as one would see from a high mountain – the fells of Cumbria were decaying into a satanic vision of so called prosperity! The Mining Industry's presence dominated many fell tops!

This picture spread over the ceiling of the caravan and great eminences were seen about a wide clear tarn. It was dark and the moon shone on high – and figures appeared – looming out of the darkness. Fleeting figures dressed in armour – climbing up to the tarn from below. There came a great cry of exaltation –

"THE TIME OF THE KING!
BRING FORTH CUMBRIA'S LOST KING!"

Sometime later the Tramp being fascinated by his dream – decided upon a point of action. Therefore one day when the dawn came slowly – and after the mists had cleared – Joe the Tramp with Dusty decided to go and head for the famous mountain lake at the head of

Grisedale. Joe was fresh and fit to begin with! After his mid-day lunch which he devoured out in the open sunlight he felt fatigued and so tired he thought of giving up his walk and return to Glen- ridding. This of course would have been the most sensible thing to do!

Foolishly however Joe the Tramp went onwards knowing the final approach to the Tarn was strenuous and soul sapping!

It was now beginning to get dark – a prospect he'd overlooked – and now the last hard-slogging pitch was upon him. But his attention was drawn to something way ahead in the distance – where a spot of light began to –

TWINKLE!

– one having roamed ahead of him. He stood and peered towards it. Finally the speck of light went out. Joe shook his head and struggled on – overcoming each jumbled boulder strewn pitch as it presented itself.

A faint pale moon hung high in the sky and then –
quite unbelievably – there ahead was the round and
sparkling surface of Grisedale Tarn. Again the speck of
light appeared!

But on this occasion it was quite near to him. The
moon then showed her brilliance from a cloudless sky
and once again the phantom-like speck of light
disappeared. Joe sat down and proceeded to wait for the
approaching dawn. The moon had been hiding – and
when it broke through the clouds Joe the Tramp – gazed
down upon the magical pool of water.

He continued to stare! The mountain lake was now a
glowing mass of silvery light! The Tramp glanced
beyond and there – well below the ridge of Saint
Sunday Crag he gasped in wonder on seeing lines of
armed warriors tramping their way towards the Lake
shouting their cries in their ancient Celtic tongue.

But more was to come and the Tramp froze in
amazement when crowds of ancient armour-clad
warriors appeared fleeing upwards in desperation from
the battle on the Raise below. Still staring in disbelief
the Tramp heard the loud cries of other warriors coming
up behind them – some of them torn and bleeding – but
all standing exhausted – a part of the remnants of King
Dunmail's army who were in full retreat downwards
toward Ulfswater.

It took the Tramp – with Dusty leading the way –
some time to trek along the road back to Glenridding
where – very wearily – he went visit his old friend Peter
Pepperson.

"You actually saw these:

APPARITIONS?

– asked Peter.

"Exactly my friend," replied the Tramp. "But I fear there is more to come!

"That seems fearful! So what do we do?" asked Peter.

"Well my friend," replied the Tramp," seeing you have met Eliza the Enchantress – and finding her a power for good – perhaps we can visit the old lady and ask her the question? But where is she to be found?"

Peter Pepperson was aware of most things around Ulfswater and the next day on a peaceful evening the two friends without Dusty who had decided she was too tired – were to be found walking along the muddy way by Brothers Water – their intention being to call on Eliza – at present their only source help in the present situation. The walk to Hartsop Hall was long and tedious – but at last the lights of the Hall began to glimmer in the distance.

But within her home the Enchantress was peering into her Magic Mirror –

and was well aware of their approach. Eliza chuckled in her usual whimsical way and waited and watched as they came near.

"There's a door within a cobbled yard at the rear of the main building, "explained the Tramp when they neared Hartsop Hall.

Looking within her Magic Mirror and on hearing and seeing the remark Eliza chuckled once again – who in a sudden mood of capriciousness began to dance around her Chamber of Spells singing –

> *"COME INTO MY PARLOUR*
> *SAID THE SPIDER TO THE FLY!"*

She continued in her madcap prancing but – knock! knock! – went the Tramp's clenched fist on the thick solid oaken door – and should the Tramp have been aware of Eliza's antics – he would have assumed the White Witch was indeed quite – '

> *MAD!*

Once again the Tramp thumped on the door – but a bright light from behind – quite confused Joe and Peter. And there stood the Eliza the Enchantress with her foxhounds straining at their leashes.

No one moved – neither Peter – nor Joe or Eliza or the foxhounds.

"How you dare enter my domain – shouted the Enchantress.

"Madam," replied the Tramp. "We are here to discuss certain events with you!"

The Enchantress swung round and faced the hounds saying:

"AWAY WITH YOU!"

The pack turned tail and with their tails flapping around they wandered away.

"Is that so Joe the Tramp – then follow me!" ordered Eliza.

They followed her through the oaken door and across a room towards an iron spiral staircase – and there the Enchantress halted saying:

"This is my secret way into the bowels of the earth!"

Peter and the Tramp looked doubtful then – down they stepped and entered a room decorated with weird magical inscriptions where Peter and Joe felt the clammy hand of fear upon them.

"Tell me what you wish to know?" said the Enchantress.

"Many things are about to come to pass," replied the Tramp," – but how will they to come about?"

"Now let me have my Looping Trooping Message Maker!"

The two friends stood quietly in a corner of the chamber when a Looping Band of Light appeared before them. Eliza asked:

"LOOPY LOO! TELL ME WHAT I SHOULD DO!"

38

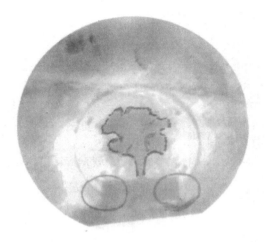

Loopy Loo the Message maker lowered its head and thought – then one of its vibrating multi-coloured message makers hovered in the air!

Eliza put on her orange pearly spectacles and began to read the message floating in the air – and said "beware of – the Time of the Ancients!

"So that's what High Hat is conscious of – and it is soon to come!" whispered Joe the Tramp in Peter Pepperson's ear

"Mm!" muttered the Enchantress who had overheard Joe's remark – and stepped over to her Magic Mirror.

The two friends peered over her shoulder – and there in the Mirror they saw a familiar sight. Beyond were the three dog-legged stretches of water of Ulfswater and near at hand the charming village of Glenridding – its main street's bustling rows of shops – and then the scene changed!

For there in the centre of the Magic Mirror stood –

A TALL KINGLY WARRIOR

– looking over the valley beneath his feet! Standing proudly as a monarch would stand surveying all the lands around him which he intended to reclaim!

"There stands King Dunmail," said Eliza, "who will return to recover his lost lands!"

FOUR

The Portal Of A Thousand And One Knocks!

Joe the Tramp hadn't been seen for many hours and this concerned Barny and Walter. Joe had long maintained the far bank of Ulfswater was little known to most people except the local folk.

One morning the two friends decided to explore this part of the dale. They left their rented cottage by the banks of Ulfswater and began walking towards Glenridding and past Patterdale where the Lake Steamers were moored. Eventually they followed a narrow road leading to the east bank of the Lake. There they began walking through a forest where they heard someone whispering!

WHISPER! WHISPER! TAP! TAP! TAP!

A small individual stepped out of the trees and put a finger to his lips and beckoned them to follow them.

"Now what?" muttered Barny.

Walter shrugged. "Well the bloke seems harmless enough – may be someone needs help!"

Instinctively they followed the short person. They continued through large clumps of shallow prickly thickets, over several narrow wooden bridges and suddenly they were out onto a road.

"I know where we are," whispered Walter. "We're now at the bottom of Kirkstone Pass!"

Led by their guide they hurriedly climbed through a gap in a line of dry stone walling and progressed over several spacious meadows until – ahead of them – loomed a precipitous wall of rock. When they shuffled nearer – a surprising window of bright light enveloped them.

"Do not worry my fellows," said the short person," – you are expected!"

"Expected?" muttered Walter.

Barny replied breathlessly –

"He probably thinks we're part of an Emergency Service!"

They walked on as it seemed – through the brightness – and much to their surprise – all around them the slightest whisper resounded like a bell.

"I think," muttered Walter, "– we're in some sort of a grotto!"

Way up high above them – much to their surprise – a haughty figure looked down upon them – one who stared at them with eyes that twinkled with amusement.

The dwarf-like person who was near at hand whispered – "He is the Chamberlain of Ulf – the Mountain King! I am sure he will help you in your endeavours."

A voice thundered down upon them.

"Troll these are not the expected ones. These are pestilences that often enter this kingdom without permission?

The short person looked perplexed.

"Did you not demand the password?"

The short person became terrified and went on his knees before the Chamberlain.

The two friends were astounded by the Chamberlain's protests but not knowing what to say to this awesome, most noble courtier before them – they merely looked about them – at the pillared hall, the rows of multi-level marbled seating, the glittering inlays of gold and silver.

The haughty figure peering down upon them began to lose his patience.

"Come now ye silent ones and follow me to his majesty the King's chambers – and we will see what he has to say!"

The Chamberlain, with the trembling small person leading the way – and with Barny and Walter following behind – they walked onwards through more curtains of dazzling light. The further they went the more the light began to change – to white, pink, scarlet, orange, yellow and green!

Finally they faced a grand stone entrance with a stout oak door studied with precious twinkling stones.

"This is the portal of a –

THOUSAND AND ONE KNOCKS!"

– uttered the Chamberlain, "– because I am a person of High Office I have to knock only once – begin Troll!

The small person (who was actually a Troll) lifted his knuckled hand and solemnly knocked upon the jewelled oak door.

The door opened without a murmur – before them shooting down into the earth was an endless flight of steps.

"You see before you," shouted the Troll:

THE STEPS OF NUMBERS!

– and only our Chamberlain knows the magic procedure - and what is more if one gives the wrong answer you may not go any further," – shouted the Troll.

"Nine times nine," yelled the Troll.

"Forty-six!" responded the Chamberlain.

"That's wrong!" shouted Barny. "Nine times nine are eighty-one."

"Things are different here!" roared the angry Chamberlain and they stepped down a step.

"Seven times seven!" yelled the Troll.

"Twenty-two!" said the Chamberlain who glared about him should anyone disagree.

"Wrong! The answer is forty-nine," whispered Barny under his breath and down they went

"Forty-four!"

"Wrong!"

"Thirty-six!"

AGAIN AND AGAIN CAME THE SILLY ANSWER!

– and so on and so on. The bottom step was reached in good time because the Chamberlain said he'd given all the correct answers.

"Just so!" agreed the Troll.

The Steps of Numbers being behind them the Troll ordered everyone to halt.

"Our noble Chamberlain will now instruct you on the important procedures when we enter the Hall of our Sovereign, Ulf the Mountain King."

"But never ever," murmured the Troll, "on any account look at –

THE SOVEREIGN'S LEFT EAR!"

"His left ear?" chuckled Walter and he and Barny were convulsed with laughter!

"Do not be insolent!" roared the Chamberlain," or you will be made to walk backwards up the Steps of Numbers nine times ninety-nine times!"

There came another long, long silence

"Prepare to enter the Noble presence of Ulf the Mountain King!" shouted the Troll.

A huge curtain of dazzling light once again appeared - but this time their colours were much more profound and suitable for only those in high office – such as gold, silver, and emerald and so on and so forth!

There appeared before them seven much taller Trolls – all in a line and each one holding a large flaming candle, set within a huge glittering gold candle holder. One of them announced:

"WE ARE THE ROYAL CANDLE BEARERS!

– bodyguards of Ulf the High King – enter on tiptoe and bow your heads before his Majesty – only speak when spoken to – otherwise keep your mouths shut!"

The two Earthlings – Barny and Walter prepared to be impressed. Before them was a huge shining throne – within the throne they saw a bundle of ermine and scarlet. Upon the bundle was a shining golden crown.

"Where is his Majesty?" blurted Walter?

"I AM HERE!"

– squeaked a timid voice!"

And from within the bundle of scarlet and ermine appeared a thin small figure.

"Oh! No more strangers Chamberlain!" said his Majesty, "– stop messing me about – and see to them yourself!"

"But Majesty!" responded the Chamberlain, "– these earthlings are here quite uninvited!"

"I'm tired!" replied Ulf the High King, "give them an ice-cream –and send them away!"

Barny and Walter were about to be have a fit of laughter.

"Earthlings remember where you are!" shouted one of the Royal Candle Bearers.

"Stop it!" shouted Ulf the timid High King. "Oh very well Chamberlain – escort us to the Royal Anteroom and I will give them a private audience!"

The whole situation proceeded – with the Royal Candle Bearers at the head of the line – followed by his Majesty King Ulf with his long gown trailing behind him – pursued by the Chamberlain and the Troll – then came the two young men laughing their heads off.

Ahead of them a huge tall, wide golden door swung open!

"You can leave us here Chamberlain – and I'll see to it – go on –

BUZZ OFF!"

The Chamberlain bowed low and the rest of the Royal group doffed their hats – the golden door closed – and the two young men were left alone with Ulf the King!

"Phew!" remarked High King Ulf mopping his brow, "that was a hot one – my Chamberlain is a right skiver and leaves all the work to me! Now then what do you want?"

"Well your Majesty," explained Barny, "nothing really – we have no real reason to be here at all – except a Troll brought us to this place!"

His Majesty put his finger to his lips and whispered something quite inaudible and walked to the golden Door and putting his ear against it –

AND LISTENED!

Everyone looked askance and King Ulf tiptoed back to them and smiled.

"Things are not what they seem – in fact I'm a prisoner here!"

"What here in your own Palace?" asked Walter.

"Exactly!" replied his Majesty. "I just blundered into this place just as you have!"

The two friends stood there quite astounded!

"Do you think a simple bloke like me could actually be a king here? The offer they made me at the time seemed too good to be true! To be dined and pampered was better than sleeping rough," replied King Ulf. "But mark my words – the situation here is a complete setup and Willie the Chamberlain is at the bottom of it!"

The statement was incredible and no one made to reply and Ulf the Mountain King pushed the gleaming golden crown to the back of his head.

"It's my belief the real king was assassinated by Willie – and I'm just a figurehead!"

"But why your Majesty?" asked Walter.

"Why indeed as you might say – but there's queer goings on around here and Willie the Chamberlain is at the bottom of it!"

"How long have you known Willie the Chamberlain?" asked Barny.

"That's the point!" replied the king. "I've just arrived here and don't really know him or anyone at all! The real Chamberlain could possibly have been someone else before I was persuaded to take this job! Perhaps this is maybe the reason for adopting me!"

His majesty collected his thoughts and explained:

"IT'S A TOPSY-TURVY WORLD HERE!

– no one knows 'what is what' or 'which is which'! In fact it is probable that Willie isn't Willie at all - and maybe someone else!"

Both Barny and Walter found the tale astounding!

"If you are correct your Majesty," urged Walter, "– you must escape!"

"And soon!" said Barny. "You don't know what they're planning is me for the chop?" – replied the frightened monarch.

"More than likely!" replied Walter.

"Let we show you the way out of this place!" replied His Majesty and pointed to a wall of rock within his private chamber. "Meet me here at this time tomorrow and I'll show you how our escape route works!"

But on the following day the King failed to arrive and threw the whole plan into chaos.

"Now what we do?" said Walter

Suddenly the Troll rushed came out of the darkness somewhere beyond shouting:

"They've got his Majesty – they have captured him!"

Barny appeared somewhat perturbed.

"Well how the blazes do we get out of the place?"

"Stand side by side with me!" ordered the Troll.

"Clap your hands three times!"

CLAP! CLAP! CLAP!

"Now turn round twice!"

TURN! TURN!

"Wait awhile!"

AND SO IT HAPPENED – THE CAVERN WALL ROLLED AWAY LIKE A CURTAIN!

They walked through the gap in the cave wall to find there was thunder in the air and high above the fells one could see flashes of light leaping from cloud to cloud. These were hardly noticed when Barny and Walter made their escape – and turned their backs on the crag face behind them.

"His Majesty can't be far behind us," said Barny, "– let's hang on here a while!"

"No," replied Walter, "I reckon he's been recaptured!"

They turned and sped down the slope and across the meadow below but turned once again to look behind them.

"I can hear someone shouting way behind us," said Walter.

"It's the King!" said Barny.

"That's not the King's voice!" replied Walter, "that's the Troll!"

"WAIT FOR ME!"

shouted the breathless Troll - running up to them.

"Where's his Majesty?" asked Walter.

"He didn't stand a chance – they almost knew he would try to escape and they could not let that happen!"

"Why not?" asked Barny.

"Because he knows their great secret!"

"Great Secret!" replied Walter.

"They are waiting for –

THE TIME OF THE ANCIENTS!"

From where they were standing the cliff behind them was consumed by light.

"Now they're after us!" moaned the Troll.

He turned only to find himself quite alone – Barny and Walter were now sprinting away like the wind! The Troll followed racing over the meadows towards the road leading to Patterdale where the Lake steamers were berthed.

The two friends halted and looked behind to observe the exhausted Troll struggling to join them. Yet – just in sight a hoard of pursuers was now racing after them. Walter with Barny close behind – they sped off once again hoping to outrun the howling crowd of assailants coming on behind.

The two friends were now exhausted and ahead of them a Lake Steamer was preparing to cast off.

"They are almost treading on my heels! – wailed the Troll running behind them.

The leading pursuer was almost upon them.

"Take that!" cried Barny and the leading assailant hurtled onto the side of the road.

The Troll and the two friends were off again – but now they were heading for the landing pier and ahead stood the gangplank onto the Steamer.

"Come on!" shouted Walter," – we'll just make it!"

– went the engines of the Ulfswater Steamer which began to sail away from the pier head.

They turned and saw their hunters had stopped short – and were standing there perplexed at the sight of their victims escaping.

Then Walter went below to join Barny and the Troll in the lounge.

"Well!" said Barny – when Walter sat down beside him, "– we managed to get out of that fix!"

Barny, Walter and the Troll all laughed as the rhythmic sound of the waves when the craft sliced through the waters! And the idyllic sight of Ulfswater under a bright placid sun – more than rewarded them until they saw the dark cloud of problems rolling and twisting upon the fells way ahead of them. But within an instant Barny, Walter and the Troll realised these were the signs of more troubles to come!

FIVE

The Second Saint Turns

The following day Joe the Tramp had arranged to meet his friend Peter Pepperson in Beacon Edge. With Dusty the Retriever leading the way – it was a tired Tramp who entered 'The George Hotel' later that morning.

"How many Saints have turned?" asked Peter.

"I really have no idea!" replied the Tramp.

Peter Pepperson took the remark quite casually and turned to see the source of laughter causing many heads to turn. One of these was the receptionist who was waving at them from the far end of the hotel lounge.

"Who's that waving at us," asked Peter.

Joe waved in return and replied –

"A friend of Walter's – Daisy Crumpet!"

"And what about yon moggy?" asked Peter Pepperson pointing to her side.

Joe turned once again and looked towards Daisy Crumpet – and there besides her sitting on the top of the Reception Desk was a rather Large Black Cat.

"Oh! My friend the cat you see over there is called Big Black Felix!" replied the Tramp, "– and what a clever puss he is!"

And so it was – and even more so! For Joe the Tramp was quite unaware – earlier that morning Big Black Felix during his usual inspection of the hotel had recognised a shady character whom he had come across once before. Big Black Felix was not aware of the person being Eduardo Plonks – a kind of shady person – who had recently arrived back from South America. Furthermore Big Black Felix was quite unaware Gertrude Primm – a similar shifty character – had returned with him.

Later when Joe and his friend Peter Pepperson had finished their chit-chat over a pint of beer and departed – and the hotel closed its doors – Big Black Felix was stretched out in his favourite chair and pretending to be asleep – but with one eye open. Gradually the lights on the ground floor dimmed and the only thing that one could hear was the tick, tock, ticking of the Grandfather Clock at the bottom of the stairs.

Time passed and presently Big Black Felix went to sleep!

SKID! RATTLE! SKID! RATTLE!

Big Black Felix opened one eye!

SKID! RATTLE! SKID! RATTLE!

Big Black Felix opened his other eye – and stretched himself.

SKID! RATTLE! SKID! RATTLE!

"What can I hear?" thought Big Black Felix – keeping his belly low – he began to stalk the suspicious sounds.

Big Black Felix stopped – and crouched even lower. Then he slinked down the passage way to where the resident's cars were parked at the rear of the hotel.

In the light of a golden moon Big Black Felix peered about him and

SNIFFED!

"Mm!" thought Big Black Felix, "– there's nothing unusual here – motor cars always have a nasty smell!" – and he began to inspect the hotel's car park.

Almost at once Big Black Felix found something highly unusual – a lump of yellow hard stuff right in the middle of the yard!

"Mm!" he thought, "I must show Daisy Crumpet this when she comes back to the Hotel."

But when the morrow came Big Black Felix was fast asleep in his favourite chair – a fact Daisy Crumpet observed when she came to work in the morning. But almost at once the Chef came into the hotel's lounge.

"High Daisy! See this heavy golden thing I've picked up – and quite by chance I nearly fell over it at the back here – in the hotel's car park!"

By this time Big Black Felix had one eye open! And how Big Black Felix – and smiled!

*****

The following day Joe the Tramp and Dusty caught the bus to the village of Pooley Bridge where Dunmallard the Mapmaker lived high upon a hill overlooking the lake and the rural community below. Because the Tramp was getting somewhat older he had some difficulty in getting over the stone wall blocking the way to the path one normally takes to climb upwards.

Huffing and puffing Joe the Tramp began the strenuous climb – but unlike his attempts before – the grassy path kept moving from side to side, this way and that way!

"The Lord help me!" grumbled the Tramp. "Whatever is the matter?"

Joe tried once more but his feet kept turning the wrong way. Instead of side to side his feet moved up and down – and the weary and confused Tramp soon discovered he was back where he started.

Joe sat down and mopped his brow – and as he did so a fierce blustery wind began to blow – and within the wind an unknown voice began to speak:

"WHAT AILS THEE JOE THE TRAMP?"

Joe couldn't believe this was happening – and began to stammer a reply.

"Who are you sir? Who is speaking?"

The blustery wind blew harder and back came the reply:

"MY NAME IS THE GUARDIAN OF THE GATE!"

The Tramp began to shiver and dither.

"WHAT IS YOUR MISSION JOE THE TRAMP?"

– asked the Guardian.

"I wish to visit my friend Dunmallard the Mapmaker!"

"WAIT AND I WILL RETURN!"

After quite some time The Guardian returned – smiled and beckoned for Joe to proceed – then the breeze blew stronger. The trees below by the river began to bend and dip – nodding their canopies as one – until the whole of the forests around Pooley Bridge became one seething mass of turmoil.

Joe and Dusty looked below where a thrashing –

WHIRLING MASS OF LEAVES AND TWIGS!

– reared upwards to where he was standing. The Tramp once again began to struggle upwards along the steep path to the top of Dunmallard Hill. Dusty turned to look downwards once again and saw the whirling twirling mass of fragments were upon him. The Tramp and his new friend was blown off their feet and carried upwards – higher and higher.

The Tramp then prepared himself for a fearsome fate when the turbulent whirling maelstrom exploded and he dived for cover. Then everything about him subsided and Joe and Dusty found themselves lying upon the ground buried within a heap of leaves and broken branches.

The unsteady Tramp raised himself and crawled and struggled to his feet and wearily stepped free into the open. There he and Dusty found themselves standing on the summit of the hill!

Quite unknowing of what was to come Joe became shrouded in darkness – a state that persisted until he became aware of bright burning candles. Around him were walls of mud and shingle. There standing before him was a solid ancient desk upon which lay an array pens, pencils etc. Behind the desk sat a cheery red faced grey bearded dwarf who spoke kindly to him and offered his hand in greeting.

Joe reached forward and took Dunmallard the Mapmaker's hand and chuckled as he replied –

"It is said that High Hat has returned!"

"And so he has my friend," replied Dunmallard. "I myself feared for your safety!"

"You refer to the maelstrom that almost did for me on the hill?" replied the Tramp.

"Ah most confusing occurrence! And you are perplexed friend Joe?"

"That I am friend Dunmallard –and as I see it High Hat was the cause of it!"

Dunmallard then saw Dusty.

"Ah what is this I see friend Joe?"

"A friend – as one may say –who has adopted me!"

The Dwarf roared with laughter and patted the Retriever.

But the Tramp did not laugh because his visit was quite meaningful.

"But I am also sorry to say friend Dunmallard –

THE SECOND SAINT HAS TURNED

But there is more to our concerns – being the strings of my puzzle will not meet as one!"

The candle light dipped as if a breeze came from somewhere.

The Tramp continued:

"Friend Dunmallard – have you heard of –

THE TIME OF THE ANCIENTS?"

The dwarf remained silent and looked over his spectacles at Joe's wrinkled face.

"Indeed I have friend Joe – but it can only happen under certain circumstances!"

"I agree friend Dunmallard – The Time of the Ancients is but an unbeliever's term for the beginning of the Celtic Year named –

SAMHAIN!

– which begins on the last day of October," explained the Tramp, " – when nature appears to be dying – seed fall in other words – and from death and darkness springs new life! And the dead pass through the veil dividing this life and the next – and sit around the living's camp fires and warms themselves!"

"And this bothers you?"

"It does so friend Dunmallard – I fear a great catastrophe is ahead of us!"

"Therefore my friend?"

"Simply this! "explained the Tramp. "The land around here is threatened by industrialisation – this is so because it is said gold has been discovered and there are likely buyers for this metal!"

"Well sort out the problem," replied Dunmallard, "– because there be no gold here – only lead!"

"The Wicked Black Wizard is behind it all – and his avarice knows no bounds and has great magic to swindle people!"

Dunmallard waited – expecting a further explanation.

"Because friend Dunmallard – Ulfswater is threatened by foreign forces – and because of this an ancient King is about to return to save his kingdom once again."

The silence occurred one again – but this time it was exceedingly profound!

"The greatest puzzle being friend Dunmallard – the crown of this ancient king has been lost and must be found – so he is rightfully able to lead his warriors!"

"I see you have not only a great problem, "replied the Dwarf, "and also a greater task ahead of you!"

"As you will have gathered friend Dunmallard – I am here to ask your advice!"

The Dwarf fumbled with his beard and thought!

"To find a lost crown? May I say – the Old Crone named Lendal is worth a visit – and also Seam Splitter might also help you – for he is adept at working within the hills and has hunted down High Hat and his Brood many times in the past."

Here came a lull in the conversation.

"I expect the two teenagers I once met here are now fully grown?"

"They are both involved in our troubles with Prince of Darkness – where there are hints of various things – namely the illegal mining for gold!"

"Here around Ulfswater my friend? replied Dunmallard. "Never – there only be some remains of lead ore! If you require more information on that score go and visit a far off place – just north of Ulfswater – and visit Dalemain a country house with a great stock of

books wherein there are means to solve every problem –
even yours friend Joe to find a lost crown!"

THE OLD CRONE OF DALEMAN

The Tramp pulled at his lip.

"As I have just suggested," replied Dunmallard, "but
unfortunately to find the answer to your troubles is
fraught with danger – should you attempt to search the
wide-ranging library at Dalemain for references and
unearth them!"

"Oh! You refer to High Hat I presume?"

"Of course friend Joe – is he not behind every evil?
Even the possibility of mining here in Ulfswater?"

"Indeed it be so!"

As they were in deep discussion the gentle sound of a
flute was heard – this began to increase in its intensity.

"Ah! friend Joe," if you hear the heightening of the
flute – may I inform you a sumptuous serving of food is
ready and awaiting us."

The Mapmaker ushered the Tramp followed by Dusty
from the chamber and onto a –

DOWNWARD SLOPING PASSAGEWAY!

– and there – were accompanied by other hungry
dwarfs who trooped lower and lower – until they

entered a bright and cheerful dining room where sparkling chandeliers beamed light all about them.

Instantly they were escorted to a place of honour at the head of a table upon which were arranged an unimaginable profusion of delicacies.

When everyone had been seated Joe – with Dusty sitting close by – listened to a short speech welcoming Joe the Tramp.

The flutes began to play once again accompanied by the rattle of cutlery and tinkling of tableware. At the end of the feast – the toasts began. Joe sat quite embarrassed when – with Dusty snuggling under the table – various compliments were heaped upon him.

Later the Dwarf together with Joe the Tramp – with Dusty wagging her tail must profusely – returned to Dunmallard's chamber where the previous discussion continued.

"Here is some more advice for you friend Joe!" said the Mapmaker. Do not overlook – Saint John's in the Vale and where above – 'tis said – the remnants of Dunmail's men retreated.

"Do you refer to –

THEIR LAST STAND?"

"May be yes! Maybe no!" replied Dunmallard. "But 'twas a revered spot for many years! Go there and see what you can discover!"

"And that is my task?"

"Possibly friend Joe – what more can a man do when the facts are not clear?"

"You speak in riddles Dunmallard!"

"There are other sources of knowledge! And as I have informed you friend Joe – and that is even though the dangers are profound – you yourself – must venture to the stately home of –

DALEMAIN

– and it is my belief you will uncover many facts previously unknown to you in its vast library – where an old Crone called Lendal may help you! But mind my friend she is feared by all who work there! Never, ever cross the Old Crone named Lendal!"

"A person so ruthless?"

"It is so my friend." replied Dunmallard. "Her life altered when as a devout Christian she was sent as a Church Missionary to the South Sea Islands – there she eventually married one of the native Chieftains whom she thought she had converted into the ways of goodness in the Christian faith!"

"And then friend Dunmallard?" replied the Tramp.

"Later somehow she became involved in local ways herself – and dabbled in witchcraft and so was consumed – over time – by Evil and its myriad way of working!"

"And she returned to here to her own country?"

"Very true friend Joe – but with an excess of immense knowledge that was eventually recorded – and much of these facts are to be found in Dalemain itself!"

"But there are many libraries that hold such things friend Dunmallard!"

"Not so my friend for such knowledge of another culture and thinking in the Black Arts are not equalled as one would unearth there in Dalemain – therefore its library may contain some powerful intelligence that we in Europe have no possible understanding! But beware my friend for it is rumoured there is a second secret library where Lendal's deepest of secrets or stored!

SIX

The Storm On The Lake -
The Third Saint Turns

Way, way down within the earth – in an immense cavern – teams of Boggarts were filling barrows with ore free spoil – then lifting them upwards onto a series of wide wooden steps. Once in place these were tipped by other gangs – one by one – into lines of oncoming swinging tubs. These continued on their way above the roaring blasts of fiery cauldrons – and eventually dumped the spoil somewhere above ground.

The air was hot – scarlet tinged – containing yellow drifting mists billowing high within the chamber's void. Choking mists seeking entry into the mouths and lungs of all the labouring Boggarts – and should the wetted scarves fall from their faces many fell unconscious or worse. In another place toiling gangs of other Boggarts ladled scalding yellow liquid into lines of casting moulds – where they were left to cool.

High Hat also joined the toil – fuelled by his ravenous greed for wealth and power. Walking along a wide walkway the Prince of All Evil cast his wicked eye over all of those slaving below. High Hat snarled and watched the moving conveyor belt carrying the lead ingots.

Eventually these reached the tunnels at the end of the cavern where the Prince of All Evil – his magic wand in his hand tapped each lead ingot as it went by him – where he muttered strange incantations.

"There Frondwagger!" he said, "– now they appear to be gold!"

"Precisely my Lord," replied High Hat's chief Boggart, "I am pleased you say so –

APPEAR TO BE GOLD"

"Very true Frondwagger," replied High Hat, "– Alchemists have striven for years to turn base metals into gold and the task has proved to be hopeless – but my magic should keep them appearing as gold forever!"

"But my Lord," replied the Chief Boggart, "– surely someone in future will discover the truth?"

"Who cares!" replied High Hat, "– by that time things will have changed and we'll be miles away!"

Then the crooks burst into raucous laughter – that spread far and wide within the chamber!

The Prince of all Evil went further and remarked –

"THE PHLOSOPHER'S STONE IS A MYTH!

– but our trick will succeed!

High Hat gazed around at the fiery sight.

"I sense the fumes from the furnaces have lessened somewhat?"

"Yes my Lord we have reinstalled another system of fans to lessen them!"

"Good man Frondwagger!"

"The old system was inefficient my Lord – and the noxious fumes were affecting our workforce – and that would mean lower production levels!"

"Excellent Frondwagger! Now free of the fumes all will be well!" replied High Hat and walked away to inspect other gangs of slaving Boggarts!

*****

Napoleon – hauling the Green Caravan – struggled against the wind while on either side of the road the lashing gale ripped branch after branch – from the topmost canopies of forest trees. As far as the eye could see – forked lightning flashed and flashed again and again across the darkening sky.

ZIG! ZIG! ZAG! FLASH!

The smooth road was shining from frequent downpours and Napoleon began to tread very warily – while Barny watched the sky above for the signs of the Boggart Brood. Yet indeed high overhead – could be Boggarts having changed their form – to a flock of crows.

CAW! CAW! CAW!

The Tramp who was humming to himself – had been thinking:

"We are entering a storm – for the lightning comes ever nearer – and what is more the way ahead seems to foretell trouble. I feel deep within my bones another Saint will turn their back upon the world!"

It was still raining when in the distance a shadowy building began to come into sight. Its lighted windows became peering eyes in the coming darkness. The golden retriever called Dusty sniffed the sodden air and snuggled near to her new found master who flicked the reins saying:

"Come on Napoleon my old friend – a little faster" – and tugged the reins once again.

DRUM! DRUM! DRUMMITY! DRUM!

Napoleon also sniffed the rain filled air and was in no mood to venture nearer. The house in the dale disturbed him. The eyes of its lighted windows held memories of bygone years when as a colt he was stabled with his mother and in the care of a stable hand – a wicked youth who repeatedly taunted him.

"Clip! Clop! Clipperty! Clop!" – at last the Mansion's gates were reached and beyond stood the stately home of –

DALEMAIN

From the top most windows of the Mansion a sullen face appeared and the wilful eyes of Lendal – the Old Crone of Dalemain – peered down upon them.

"Clip! Clop! Clip! Clop!" again and again Joe the Tramp flicked the reins and Napoleon – his head down – walked slowly towards the stately home's main entrance. The atmosphere was wrong and Napoleon's horse-sense told him so.

The Tramp hauled on the bridle when he and Barny let themselves down onto gravelled surface of the road –

and Dusty – her eyes sparkling jumped down after them. With the golden retriever leading the way – they walked towards where a servant stood waiting to speak to them before the main door of the stately home. The man with an apologetic nod of his head pointed to the back of the building – then quietly returned into the house.

The Green Caravan swept round into the rear yard and before the entrance a tall lady appeared before them. A sombre woman completely attired in black – who frowned upon them.

"Did you not read the notice at the gate!" she growled, "– No Hawkers or Travelling Folk allowed beyond this Point!"

The rain began to increase and thunder claps rent the air.

"Madam!" replied the Tramp brushing away the rain streaming down his face ," – we are neither of these – but here to request admittance in order to look for information held in Dalemain' s famous library?"

The glare from the intrusive old lady's gaze continued.

"Wait here!" she snapped and disappeared into the house.

Somewhere within the house a bell rang. There followed a scampering of feet and a tall smartly dressed Butler stepped before them with two assistants close behind. One of them began to speak on the Butler's behalf:

"May we invite you all into our Master's apartment – please allow a groom to take charge of your horse and caravan!"

Napoleon was led away and Joe the Tramp holding Dusty by her lead – with Barny walking behind them – were shepherded into the grand house by one of the Butler's assistants. Keeping just ahead of them their guide escorted them to where he stopped before a pair of high white double-doors and tapped three times. There must have been a silent response – the door swung back and they were ushered into a large high-ceilinged chamber.

Lines of marble pillars surrounded the walls and before them was an impressive long desk. Behind a high-backed swivel chair where plumes of cigar smoke twirled upwards. The door behind them closed silently – and swivel chair turned around – and there sat a plump gentleman with a Roman-nose.

Barny's eyed opened wide and whispered:

"His nibs?"

"Greetings gentlefolk! Allow me to introduce myself!" announced the speaker – with a enormous flourish of his hand: I am 'His Nibs' the head of –

THE ORGANISATION

Joe accepted the announcement – but Barny and Dusty became bewildered and nervous on hearing the name of such a secret society.

With a swift wave of his hand 'His Nibs' indicated three armchairs set by his desk. When the three visitors had settled themselves (which included Dusty) the gentleman with the Roman-nose coughed. Then – with a delicate gesture – he placed his smoking cigar upon an ancient ceramic tray.

Joe and Barny felt quite apprehensive – especially when a line of short people entered wearing black hooded gowns. Barny peered within the black cowls and saw wide staring eyes, frightful slobbering lips and the hint of long wide ears.

"Boggarts!" he murmured.

Joe the Tramp was equally startled by the obvious presence of the Brood – yet neither he nor Barny betrayed their feelings.

More Black Hooded Boggarts appeared carrying shining metal teapots, milk, sugar and delicacies on glowing yellow metal trays. These were placed on small tables near to where he Tramp and Barny were sitting.

Dusty began to growl and peered cautiously around the room – whereupon many other Black Hooded Boggarts entered the chamber. The man who had risen from his chair suddenly became attired in a black hooded gown and appeared to become somewhat larger and taller. The entire room was now crammed with members of the Boggart Brood.

From the rear of the chamber a door opened – then silently as if of its own accord – it closed.

CLICK!

Someone attired in the blackest of midnight black clothing slowly shuffled into the room to stand close by 'His Nibs.'

The lady in Midnight Black stared fixedly at the three friends seated before her. There she stood – or hovered slightly – and her fierce gaze increased.

"May I enquire about your mission," she asked," – which I assume to be something connected with our famous library!"

The Tramp thought it better to be diplomatic with this unknown lady.

"That is so madam," he replied," for we are here to ask permission to search your libraries for certain information needed to save the beauty of Ulfswater and the surrounding homesteads among the fells!"

"What a noble task!" replied the Black Witch called Lendal (with rather a smirk upon her face,) "– if you would care to follow me I will take you to where you may begin your searching."

Lendal the Old Crone smiling sweetly led them up a rather Grand Staircase – where the carpeted floor was soft to tread upon – and the red velvet banisters were soft to the touch. Finally the walk ended on a landing where the corridors on either side shot off in either direction. The Old Crone still smiling ever so sweetly led the way into a side-room – one of many on the corridor – where a short wooden staircase led upwards and ended at a small trapdoor – through which Lendal went from sight.

"Come through my dears – in here you will find a mass of shelving containing thousands upon thousands of learned volumes!"

Once through the trapdoor (Dusty was the first to shoot up the ladder) they were amazed to find a very large area as one would find in a city library – where bookcase upon bookcase sped off in all directions. There they turned to their guide but –

LENDAL HAD GONE!

"That's all we need!" moaned Barny, "without her help where do we start?"

The lights about them dimmed and a mighty thunderclap resounded around the bookshelves making a –

MYRIAD PAGES RUFFLED!

"We must keep the reason for our visit always to the forefront of our thinking,"

announced the Tramp." Lord knows what may happen – remember we are now in the Presence of Supreme Magic! Therefore keep your minds on the task ahead!"

While Dusty who seemed frisky went wandering around the Library – Barny and Tramp began the search.

"What subjects do we look for?" asked Barny. "There are loads here –Numismatics, Entomology, Clog Dancing, Psychology, Neurosciences and more and more?"

"Try Magic or Magicians or maybe Witchcraft!" the Tramp replied.

Book after book was searched for Magical Information – Spells of the Ancient Egyptians, Spells of the Aztecs, Ancient Spells of China, of the Mongols and much, much more – and every time each book was opened the pages went blank!

For a very long time nothing – the only sounds heard were the slithering of the searcher's feet below the Library's endless rows of shelving.

Barny my boy!" shouted the Tramp,"– we are in trouble!"

"You're telling me Joe!" replied the young man, "every book I choose has nothing but blank pages!"

"Keep looking friend Barmy we may yet discover something of value!"

But this was not the case – for no matter where they explored within the whole Library all the pages within the books were –

BLANK!

"It's the Old Crone herself doing this mischief!"

They stopped their searching and retired to a corner of the chamber and sat down on some chairs.

"Well now what do we do my young friend?"

"First of all let's find Dusty," replied Barny, "– she's been away some time and probably finds herself lost!"

The search for the Golden Retriever began – and because the rows of bookshelves were placed in parallel lines – making it easy to search between the gaps – it was realised the dog was nowhere to be found. Therefore they began to look for the exit door – and failed to find one.

"This is stupid!" grumbled Barny," there must be door somewhere or how on earth did we get in?"

"Magic my boy!" chuckled the Tramp. "Did I not tell you of our being in the Presence of Supreme Magic!"

Barny began to laugh!

"I am so pleased my young friend," replied the Tramp, "you see the funny side of things!"

BUT NOT FOR LONG!

For there came a shriek of laughter and there above them standing in an apse high in the wall was – the Wicked Old Crone!

"So!" she crooned – and rubbing her hands together in spiteful anger. "Now I have more surprises for you all!" The wicked Old Crone drifted down to stand near them. "Therefore follow me!"

As if they were being propelled by an unknown hand they followed her – through every barrier – either wall or bookcase or anything at all – and found themselves standing within another room full of bookshelves. Barny and the Tramp looked around them and the two friends began to tremble with fear

"As you see! "said the Wicked Black Witch, "you are within another Library!"

MY SECRET LIBRARY!

This came as shock to Barny – but not Joe the Tramp whom had remembered Dunmallard's warning –

"There is a second secret Library where Lendal's deepest secrets are stored!"

"You are here on a fool's errand – for you are already aware of the secret you wish to find!"

"So here you will both remain until you – rot!"

Back in Ulfswater Joe the Tramp and Barny had not been missed and it wasn't until Dusty returned quite alone that folk began to be concerned. Walter and the Troll found the Golden Retriever waiting patiently when they returned to the rented cottage by the Lake. The news spread fast and it wasn't long before Peter Pepperson arrived together with the Mountain Rescue Team.

"I don't believe this!" murmured Peter Pepperson. "Joe the Tramp disappearing for a second time!"

"They were going to visit Dalemain," replied Walter, "– a country house on the way to the main highway."

"I've passed the spot many times," replied Peter. "Was their visit something special?"

"You should know Peter," replied Walter, "the whole of Ulfswater are expecting something peculiar to happen in the near future!"

There the discussion ended and everyone – including Dusty – boarded the Lake Steamer and sailed for the landing stage at Poole Bridge. Then a great storm began when huge waves battered the lake steamer.

"This storm is no coincidence!" blurted Walter sarcastically. "All should be well aware who has conjured up this filthy weather!

HOOVEY! HOOVEY! HOOVEY!

The Lake Steamer's prow dipped and rose in the troughs of the waves! How the spray engulfed those aboard time after time!

HOOVEY! HOOVEY! HOOVEY!

Many on board were ordered below and only Walter was allowed on deck.

The experience on ship began to disturb everyone – so unusual was the sudden thunderstorm. Never had anyone experienced such a northerly gale. The shores of Ulfswater appeared to rise and fall in an unprecedented manner!

UP! DOWN! UP! DOWN! UP! DOWN!

Then Dusty – having sneaked away from Lounge – trotted up the stairway and was soon snuggling up to Walter sitting in the prow of the ship. There he sat looking for floating debris – for a collision with a floating log would make matters worse!

HOOVEY! HOOVEY! HOOVEY!
CRASH!

– a rampant wave hit the Steamer's bow sideways-on – catapulting Walter onto a wide coil of rope and down the hatch to where others were sheltering.

HOOVEY! HOOVEY! HOOVEY!

The gale then shifted to the north-west and the steersman fought like mad to bring the prow into the wind. Gradually and ever so slowly they were once again facing into the wind.

HOOVEY! HOOVEY! HOOVEY!

The landing stage at Poole Bridge came ever nearer but time after time the steersman failed to judge the rise and fall of the waves. Finally those on the pier threw ropes and those aboard – now saturated with the rain – managed to secure the ship to shore.

Dusty the Golden Retriever was the first ashore – and made off towards the pier head. Walter and Grieg and the Mountain Rescue team dashed off after her.

CLATTER! CLATTER! CLATTER!

Iron-shod soles sounded on the rough road. Way ahead of them the bitch raced towards the Country House of Dalemain – now appearing bright and shiny in the mid-day sun.

Walter and Grieg stopped – way ahead of them the Mountain Rescue Team bounded after Dusty. Eventually the team neared Dalemain – where standing patiently – her tail wagging excitedly – she waited for the others to catch up.

Eventually Walter and Grieg reached the gates and began a slow lumbering trot towards the rear of the Mansion. There a gaggle of rescuers were hammering upon its rear entrance where they looked about for any sign of the bitch and once again they began to look for her. They turned on hearing the –

YAP! YAP! YAP! YAPPING!

– sound of a frightened animal and found Dusty trapped in an open storm drain.

YAP! YAP! YAP! YAPPING!

"Dusty!" yelled the Walter. There – lodged within the drain – among a mass of fallen debris the Golden

Retriever was struggling. Walter soon cleared the way ahead – and he and Grieg and an excited Dusty ventured beyond into the darkness!

SEVEN

Millican

The mist bedevilling the view over the lake had cleared – and Millican – the Hermit of Castle Rock looked startled. Way, way, below – three strangers were walking along the road towards Castle Crag – his isolated home. He watched them closely when they halted and looked upwards to the Crag's summit.

The Hermit continued to look down – narrowing his eyes to peer more closely. The sight was quite a normal experience on the highways and byways – when many walkers trod the Lakeland roads during the summer and autumn months.

Local folk had noticed The Hermit on the nearby fells for the last five years – although no one knew his name or from where he came. And much more – he avoided company when walking over the fells in any season. Hence he was known solely as The Hermit.

Eventually the three strangers disappeared from sight – and although he didn't realise it at the time they were beginning to climb upwards along the tortuous and tricky path to the summit of his home – Castle Rock. Millican shrank back and tiptoed silently out of sight yet still observing the three unfamiliar people.

"Well," gasped one when they reached the top, "– I'm past my days for antics such as these!"

The two younger men with him were also panting with exertion and made no answer – and stopped to stand admiring the view. There they remained catching their breath looking at the panorama around them. The view was remarkable – seeing a portion of the three dog-legged stretches of Ulfswater.

"Now what do we do?" said one

"A good question!" chuckled the taller stranger.

They looked about them possibly to glimpse of the presence of the person they had come to visit – the Hermit of Castle Rock – but Millican was still hiding.

The tall stranger – who was obviously the leader – together with the two young men – began to wander around the fell.

"There was a time," remarked the group leader, "– when mining was the craze around this spot – and subsequently many trees were felled."

By this time the two younger men had strayed away – peering here and there trying to make sense of the piles of rock and the gaping holes scattered all about them. A short way ahead they saw –

THE FOUR LARGE HEADSTONES

– Standing neatly in an orderly row – contrasting with the boulder field around them.

They turned and waved as the tall stranger came over to them.

"– What an oddity!" he remarked indicating the four stones.

The background behind the Four Headstones was impressive. From north to south stretching in sequence were The Great and Little Mell Fells, Gowbarrow Fell, Place Fell and other fells south of High Street.

"Breath-taking!" said one looking at view

"True man true!" said another.

The taller stranger remained silent taking in the vista before them.

Millican, from where he was standing, was suspicious of the newcomers – who immediately looked in his direction. The Hermit was surprised, yet smiled and walked hesitantly across the rough mountain path to greet them!

They shook hands and then there followed lots of questions.

"We approached Castle Rock and noticed a strange figure standing like a – Sentinel – there way above you!" they remarked pointing a finger towards the top of the fell.

"Greetings to you strangers," replied the Hermit making no reply saying –

"Come to my campfire and warm yourselves – even on a hot summer's day the evenings on high gets chilly!"

The three strangers came nearer rubbing their cold hands together.

"My name is Millican and indeed the vision you perceived," replied The Hermit, "– I myself have seen many times – not just around here but in other place among the fells – therefore you may well ask questions!"

The strangers – who were mining prospectors – nodded in agreement but remained silent.

"It is my belief what you saw," said Millican, "– is an apparition of –

DUNMAIL THE LAST KING OF CUMBRIA!"

The prospectors accepted this thoughtful statement quite calmly.

"Therefore – uneasy lies the head," laughed Millican, "that wears the crown?"

"How is that?" replied the tall prospector.

"Well!" replied Millican. "Obviously where is the crown to be found? If the rumours are true, King Dunmail is to lead his warriors once again! Having said that – a King is not a King at all without his crown!"

The Hermit stirred the campfire with a branch of a tree – one of many stacked by him.

"It is my contention, the apparition is the key to this mystery – being an example of – the Natural

Manipulation of Time – and within it the crown of gold must be evident!"

The fire crackled and flickered – casting shadows far and wide. The face of the crag behind them glimmered revealing its shadowed cracks and indentations.

"May I be frank with you Millican?" said the tall prospector. "If our application to mine hereabouts is permitted, the Headstones will be removed – therefore it is best the crown be found before this happens!

Once again Millican nodded and remained silent.

"The four headstones?" asked the tall prospector, "– can they be explained?"

Millican shrugged his shoulders saying, "– the stones appeared when the forests roundabout were cleared!"

"It is also my opinion," said Millican, "there was battle on the border of ancient Cumbria – the King's forces scattered in all directions – but I maintain the remnants of much of the King's forces retreated here – and buried whatever they were carrying!"

"And marked the spot with four headstones?"

The Hermit smiled and raised his arms up high.

"Well my friend," replied Millican, "what more could it be? Perhaps we will never know – this area has been cleared and the four headstones probably resettled?"

Millican picked up another log and threw it onto the fire.

"Therefore Millican," asked the tall prospector, "– is it possible the body of the King lies beneath one of the headstones?"

"Maybe!" replied Millican, "– the headstones have been resettled – but where were they before? Finding it would be a tremendous task!"

The Hermit reached casually over the fire to where one of the suspended billycans had begun to steam.

"One of them will be well stewed," he said, "– why not try my special brew?"

They all chatted amongst themselves – well into the night – and dawn was breaking when they shook hands and made their farewells. Millican stood watching them as they descended to the road below the mountain

There he stood still wondering what the future would bring!

"Prospectors here in the Lake District!"

It was a worried Millican who turned and looked behind him and upwards to top of the fell – and there standing stiffly as if on guard was a,

THE CROWNLESS SENTINEL

– gazing over the lands that were once his own!

*****

Once they'd emerged from the conduit, Walter, Grieg and Dusty waited awhile to become used to a sombre dimly lighted cellar where – around the walls stood many bulky cardboard packages.

"Wine casks!" announced the Grieg – but Dusty was sniffing around the chamber – her tail wagging vigorously.

They turned to see her pawing at a door in the cellar wall. Walter walked over and pulled it slightly ajar and

there ahead were a flight of wooden steps. Cautiously –
with a hand on Dusty's collar, Walter pulled the door
open – and without hesitation the Golden Retriever leapt
forward, pulling the lead behind her and clambering
away to the top of the stairs.

The room above was obviously a store room with
more wooden packing cases and empty tea chests
stacked one upon the other around the room. But there
was no sign of Dusty. Walter and Grieg were struggling
to decide what to do next – when the bitch's fierce
barking and the distant sound of banging drew their
attention to somewhere beyond. They ran blindly from
room to room and quite by chance blundered into a huge
majestic hallway. The panels of the nearby doors at the
main entrance where bulging and heaving from the
constant pounding by those trying to break in.

DRUM! DRUM! DRUMMERTY! DRUM!

Walter and Grieg felt the evil presence of the Brood
and dashed forward and pulled back the bolts! The door
opened and the rescuers poured into the vast hallway
and stood entranced by the magnificent scene around
them. Three tiers of balconies curved the foyer and all
glistened with light – but Walter was unruffled and
quite aware of something unpleasant lurking somewhere
above.

The group of rescuers stepped silently up the stairway
to reach the first balcony and looked around to the left
and to the right. Nothing could be seen. Nothing stirred!
Not even a whisper or a snore from a dormouse sleeping
soundly in her hole in the skirting board the intruders

quietly tip-toed by. A clock chimed the hour somewhere around them – and not having discovered the Boggart Brood they began to tip-toe upwards to the second balcony – only to discover once again there wasn't a Boggart in sight.

Walter and Grieg with Dusty trotting ahead of most of the rescuers following behind – reached the third balcony where Walter unthinkingly brushed something away from his face. Grieg began to itch and scratched his head – and others following – began to scratch, and scratch, and scratch!

Hundreds of shiny threads began dropping from somewhere above – and onto the rescuers behind Walter and Grieg. The Troll looked down and there upon the carpeting were scurrying forms with many legs.

Dusty yelped and began prancing about!

"SPIDERS!"

yelled Walter, "– thousands of them!"

From somewhere about the voice of the Old Crone of Dalemain rang out – snarling, and vengeful!

"SEE TO THEM MY BEAUTIES
– DRIVE THEM FROM THE HOUSE!"

Grieg looked behind – and dozens of the Ulfswater folk began to shout and streams of endless numbers of spider threads began descending from above.

"Help!" screamed one lady, "They're in my hair!"

The folk packed together in the passage began to panic – pushing and shoving others aside in order to escape the monstrous spiders clinging to their clothing.

"Let me out!" shouted one gentleman, "– they're getting under my clothing!"

The rescue attempt became a rout. Many fought each other to rid themselves of the spiders!

The mass of people swayed this way and that way, from one side to the other side! And in and out of the motley rout, the bitch called Dusty kept hopping about!

"Down the stairs and head for the door!" shouted a panic stricken rescuer.

And everyone followed and made for the front entrance – and kicking and scratching, the whole mass of rescuers were out of the house and haring for the Mansion's gates and the road beyond!

However, the commotion outside the Country House went unheard by Walter and his two companions Grieg and Dusty.

Quite by chance they had blundered into the Stately Home's kitchens, where a convenient exit to the open air had obviously been necessary. But on entering the kitchen they had been baffled by what they discovered.

"Look what I've found!" gasped Grieg holding something for all to see. "Look: hanging on this cupboard door – Barny's anorak!"

"What?" Walter shouted! "Well don't just stand there! Open the door!"

The Troll pulled the door open – and there sat Joe the Tramp and Barny – bound and gagged!

Walter dashed forward and pulled gags from their faces!

"What kept you!" mumbled Barny.

"Just so!" chuckled the Tramp, "things have been a little hectic around this quarter!"

Walter and the Troll spent little time waiting for explanations and within minutes the two prisoners were hustled out of the kitchens and into the open air. It was now early morning and the Manor was clothed in mist, when they come across Napoleon happily munching hay in one of the stalls in the stables and parked nearby was the Green Caravan.

"Where is Dusty?" asked Walter.

"Search me!" replied Barny. "Once she saw the spiders – she was off like a bullet from a gun!"

"YAP! YAP! YAP!"

There came Dusty sleepy-eyed coming out of Napoleon's stall – wagging her tail profusely. Within minutes all were aboard the Green Caravan and heading as silently as possible towards the main road – and then beyond to Ulfswater.

But watching from an attic window, high in the stately home of Dalemain, was Lendal the Wicked Old Crone laughing like a drain –

"Your fool's errand is over!" she cackled. "You return with nothing – except what you are already aware of –

KINGS AND THINGS!"

And Lendal the Wicked Old Crone – laughed and laughed and laughed!

EIGHT

'Find The Crown Of Gold!'

After the three friends returned from the abortive venture to Dalemain House – Joe the Tramp went away somewhere with Dusty without any explanation.

"He'll have gone away to visit Peter Pepperson," remarked Walter "To discuss 'Kings and Things' - the problem that's always on his mind!"

"I agree," replied Barny," – the three word puzzle must be important – or the Wicked Old Crone wouldn't have mentioned it – and remember she was so sure of herself and had the nerve to laugh about it!"

They sidled along by the waterside and merged with a large crowd of tourists and their families waiting to board a Lake Steamer. The puzzle revealed by Lendal was now forgotten.

"It's a queue for a lake steamer," said Barny.

"Well something must be wrong because they're all holding tickets and no one is being allowed aboard."

Ahead of them the crowd was restless! Heads were turning! Hands were gesticulating! Folk were turning their backs and walking away! The clatter feet upon the pier resounded!

Barny was just about to make a comment when Walter took his arm and motioned him to shush!

"LADIES AND GENTLEMEN!"

– explained a uniformed figure, " it is with regret I have to inform you the steamer's locomotive power is in need of a suitable mechanic – his absence is due to sickness. May I ask if there is anyone here competent enough to help us?"

Walter sprang to life!

"I can give you a hand sir" he shouted. "I've received training in Marine Engineering!"

"Come aboard sir! " responded the Captain.

The two friends made their way through the crowd and were welcomed aboard the Lake Steamer - but Walter was the only one allowed into the engine room. People were still waiting to embark and the seamen on deck were becoming very impatient. But within half an hour Walter was back on deck with a beaming smile all over his face and the Captain followed behind him.

"Your friend was so quick to find the fault. "said the Captain to Barny, "– and should he wish to have a temporary job let him –

COME ABOARD AND BE WELCOMED!"

Barny soon realised Walter was so pleased who explained the fault was only a minor one – but the intricate explanation that followed confounded Barny - who quickly changed the subject.

Walter went below while Barny stayed on deck for the entire journey to the pier near Pooley Bridge - sitting contentedly watching the wake of the steamer cut through the calm surface of the lake.

Barny idly looked about him at the crowd of people doing as all were doing - admiring the beauty of the fells about them and at the same time gossiping about what they were seeing.

Then who should emerge on deck but the Troll.

"Here I am Barny!" said the Troll saluting. "– a Lake Steamer's Entertainment Office – 'Grieg' Able Seaman First Class!"

"Well Able Seaman Grieg – how on earth did you get the Job?"

"Remember! We were fleeing from the mob and I was the only one to escape!"

"Well of course you were - I remember now!"

"OK Barny – but I went below and began to tinkle on the piano in the lounge."

"Well some chap came along and asked me to continue playing – and from then on everyone began to clap – then the Captain appeared and offered me a job as a piano player!"

"What a splendid uniform you are wearing!"

"Don't make me blush Barny" replied Grieg rather sheepishly.

Suddenly Barny's gaze alighted upon the face of a familiar person seated opposite him on the starboard side of the steamer – the same mop of unruly black hair – the shifty eyes above a scruffy dark suit!

"EDUARDO PLONKS" –

- muttered Barny

"I'm sorry Grieg," he remarked, "- but I've got something in hand – but I'll see you later!"

Just as Grieg went below the crowd on the steamer were waiting to disembark - Walter had come on deck and the Captain was shaking his hands saying:

"I have plenty of room aboard for you young man – come any time for a job this summer!"

When the Lake Steamer docked at the pier near Pooley Bridge - Eduardo Plonks was nowhere to be seen. Barny and Walter were carried along by the crush of people who were striving to get onto the gangplank. To make matters worse a line of seamen carrying large wooden packing cases – were also determined to get onto the landing stage.

After much hustle and tussle in stepping on the quay - the two young men walked on towards the main road leading to Pooley Bridge – and there in a line at the side of the road where two golden vans - parked ready with their rear doors wide open. Barny and Walter stopped and stared when the seamen carrying the wooden cases loaded them into the vans – but there was a third man helping them - one with a mop of black unruly hair – with shifty eyes above, a scruffy dark suit Eduardo

Plonks – then stepped within the vehicle just before the doors were slammed shut and the vans sped off in the direction of Beacon Edge.

"Well what a revelation!" joked Barny, "- three packing cases, the crook Eduardo Plonks and two Golden Vans waiting for the loot!"

They turned and began to walk after the vans towards Beacon Edge. By this time they were beginning to feel tired. It was getting late in the afternoon – and they realised they had a few miles to travel. Nevertheless on they went – their walking boots echoing about them!

"Clomp! Clomp! Clomp!" - echo after echo resounding about them.

"DRUM! DRUM! DRUMMETY! DRUM!"

- came familiar sounds! They turned and looked back!

Their ungainly manner, their wide snaring eyes shocked them -

"BOGGARTS!"

- yelled Barny - and off they shot down the road to Beacon Edge!

Finding a fresh surge of energy they turned to race ahead of the pursuing Boggart Brood. On and on they galloped keeping the evil scourge behind them.

The way ahead of was clear but behind them it was a different story. The Brood were now leaping in among the trees scattered by the wayside – trying to cut them off from the safety of the straight road ahead in leaps and bounds

The energy of the Brood seemed endless – and yet the two young men continued to keep ahead. Experience told them the road wound around a bend covered in undergrowth. Realising they must take a short cut across the curve to keep ahead - their need to achieve this seemed impossible at the time.

On and on they raced and they quickly realised they were now exhausted.

"See that tall flat rock ahead lying by the roadside?" gasped Walter. "That would be high spot to fend them off!"

At that moment a stream of traffic was approaching - forcing them to the edge off the road – seizing this moment to gain the high ground - they jumped up the nearby grassy slope looming before them and swiftly reached the top of a tall rock above.

The scene below them was menacing when the odious Boggart Brood began to creep upwards towards them – and the two friends knew they were easy prey – and stood back to back – ready to fight to the end!

At that moment there came a snuffling sound from above. Barny looked upwards to the top of the cliff – and there in line on the edge of the rock face - he observed a line of – bright eyed foxhounds!

- all peering curiously down upon them. At that moment in time neither the Boggarts - nor the young men - or the foxhounds moved or blinked.

The howling and growling of the hounds made such a hullabaloo and it became so loud – that later it was said it was heard for miles and miles. Then - just as suddenly - a face appeared looking down upon them -

"ELIZA!"

- shouted the two young men!

Once again no one stirred – until a few of the fox hounds began to nose their way downwards from the top of the cliff. The effect on the Brood below was instantaneous and in an instant the Brood were off like a bolt of lightning back along the way whence they had come.

Eliza the Enchantress beckoned the two young men to climb upwards – and this they accomplished in a long arduous ascent where Eliza was quick to ask questions.

"What is this I see? Two young men surrounded by the Evil Brood?"

In a state of near exhaustion Barny and Walter began to offer – what to them at the time - seemed to be a long complicated explanation.

"Enough!" shouted the Enchantress. "What you have said and what I have witnessed is enough for even the slow witted to comprehend!"

She stared to where the Boggarts had fled and looked the other way towards the Pass.

"Mm!" she mused,"- the road to Beacon Edge is clear – therefore -

GET YOU GONE!"

- as quickly as you may!"

She turned and without the slightest sign of farewell – Eliza the Enchantress - followed by her loyal foxhounds – vanished into the woods beyond.

It was very late in the day when the two friends walked into the centre of Beacon Edge and being at that time quite depleted of energy and thoughtfulness - they simply walked into The George Hotel and sat down somewhat exhausted in the front lounge.

An hour later after having had something to eat and drink - and following closely behind Barny – Walter tiptoed to the top floor of the hotel and then a short distance down the passageway he stopped outside a certain room – and gently opened the door.

The next morning after a perfect night's slumbering Barny and Walter stepped confidently down the stairs and ordered breakfast. At that moment many of the hotel staff was away on holiday and those remaining were so busy no one seemed to notice them. But tucked away in one corner of the dining room whom should they see but Eduardo Plonks, his black unruly hair, his shifty looks and his scruffy old suit gave him away when the crook went down the passage way and out into the hotel car park

Walter was about to pass the toast rack to Barny when they heard the roar of a vehicle's engine – by the slamming of doors – and a toot-toot-toot on the horn – and away went the vehicle to wherever it was destined.

*****

Joe the Tramp had been visiting the Pepperson's to discuss the puzzle made known by Lendal. However when they left the house no definite solution had been reached. Peter and his wife stood at the garden gate and waved goodbye until he vanished within the fog.

With Dusty in the lead Joe pressed on regardless and as soon as he entered Glenridding was amazed at the number of villagers standing around gossiping.

"Now what?" he thought.

Joe however saw someone he'd spoken to previously and asked about the hubbub.

"Well haven't you heard?" replied the old gentleman. "There's a lot of Chinese folk around and as far I can make out – they are here for some kind of meeting!"

A large group of oriental people from Chang Low had arrived and were now staying in "The Glenridding Hotel.' Many folk had previous knowledge of their arrival and were gathered around the hotel's entrance.

After some hesitation the Tramp and Dusty entered the hotel and once inside crossed the thick carpeted foyer to where many folk stood gossiping. Near at hand was a tall shiny metallic doorway. Standing on either side were two smart lady attendants who smiled at the Tramp and gestured for him to enter.

Many delegates were already sitting quite contentedly awaiting the chairman's welcoming address from the raised platform ahead of them. Joe peered closely at one particularly fat plump female who appeared to come from nowhere wearing a pair of large black spectacles and upon her head wore an enormous outlandish black hat with a large peacock's feather pinned to its brim.

"GERTRUDE PRIMM!"

- thought the Tramp! But where is Eduardo Plonks – where there's Gertrude Primm there is usually Mr Plonks!"

Sitting as they were among the vast number of people present and merging completely with them Joe settled back in his seat and Dusty sat proudly on a seat beside him they waited for things to happen. Mrs Gertrude Primm stepped forward and welcomed everyone.

"It is a great pleasure to see you all here today – even more so having travelled so far to buy our gold!" and everyone began to clap!

"Therefore I can assure you this occasion will not be disappointing. Everything is ready for those members who are to offer their signatures!"

The meeting lasted around thirty minutes and was presently at an end. Those who were to sign the agreement were called upon by Gertrude Primm to witness their signatures.

When the Tramp and Dusty left the room they walked to the banks of the Lake Ulfswater and Joe began to think things over.

"The Time of the Ancients could be said to be part of the Celtic Year," mused the Tramp."And the first festival is known as Samhain!

And that means it's not too far ahead - around the last day of October and a time of the Celtic year of:

MISRULE AND DISOBEDIENCE!"

– when the veil between this world and the other world is no longer a barrier.

The Tramp continued to study the problem.

"OK," he mused. "Well – putting it simply – the Prince of all Evil must have a surprise waiting for us!"

The Tramp continued to ponder -

"When the morrow arrives I'll be gone and consult Mad Eliza the Enchantress of Hartsop Hall!"

The following day was blustery. Walking by the woods along the track leading to where the Enchantress lived was quite hazardous. Branches of all sizes were being constantly wrenched away from the trees by the high winds sweeping over the lake

But the Enchantress who was well aware of High Hat's manipulating had been attending to other business in various parts the country – but now she had returned. One morning she went below to her workshop and looked into her Magic Mirror – only to find it was clouded

Eliza hurried away and brought back a special potion and proceeded to clean it and the Mirror sprang to life at once!

There within the Mirror the face of High Hat appeared within a dark cavern with his Magic Wand in his hand She looked closely to see him tapping something – tapping each one of a line of lead ingots moving along a long conveyor belt - when in an instant they looked like gold. At first the Enchantress was baffled and could make little sense of what was happening. Eliza reached up to a high shelf - where many books on Magic stood in row upon row.

"Ah!" she mused let me see what he is up to!"

Eliza took down a very thick red volume – and flipped through the pages - page after page looking for a special incantation.

"Ah!" she crooned,"- so that's what he's up to!

MAKING LEAD LOOK LIKE GOLD"

"I will stop him in his tracks – when I cast a special spell upon him."

The Enchantress turned and looked around her.

"Now where is my special wand?" said she then there it appeared in her hand!

there it appeared in her hand.

With the Magic Wand in one hand and looking at the appropriate spell lying upon the bench before her Eliza looked into her Magic Mirror and gloated

- then as quick as lightning – a hand shot out of the mirror and snatched the book of spells! Eliza was speechless when the book of spells

"VANISHED FROM SIGHT!"

All that day Eliza the Enchantress was moody and ill at ease – at losing her special book of spells – but High Hat was ecstatic and held the book in his hands. The Black Wizard was extremely delighted and gloated over the volume knowing that no one could prevent his fraudulent swindle of his selling lead as gold. Who would not be deceived? For – as the Ancient Egyptians believed gold is the flesh of the Gods and would last for Eternity!

At about this time Joe the Tramp was walking alone (Dusty was tired and was sleeping in the Green

Caravan) down the muddy lane towards Hartsop Hall. The Tramp knew a great problem had to be solved and only the Enchantress could solve it!

Ahead of him the sombre outline of the Hall began to appear – and the Tramp fixed his eyes upon its ghostly silhouette –so much so the aged Tramp began to stumble on the potholed track – his trousers now saturated with its brimming pools of muddy water. Joe steadied himself from time to time by the simple act of coming to a halt – fixing his attention on the destination that must be attained.

Eventually after much stumbling the unsteady aged Tramp stood before the entrance of Eliza's residence. It was dark in the small cobbled yard and Joe had to feel with his hands to find the huge brass knocker set upon the door. The Enchantress was slumbering at the time but when the Tramp's fingers touched its surface the Enchantress was awake in a flash!

Her wild staring eyes focussed immediately – and she instantly grabbed her dressing gown and miraculously as it may seem to float down the stairs–- and opened the creaking door – and there stood Joe the Tramp.

The old man looked exhausted!

"Sit you down!" said she, "– rest awhile!"

The Enchantress turned and went from sight – and almost at once there she stood with a brimming bowl of hot soup and fist full of brown crusty bread. She stood back and watched the Tramp enjoy the meal that would revive him.

Shortly they were in deep conversation –

"Madam the task ahead of us is enormous – and High Hat has all the means he needs to carry out his outrageous plans!"

"Say no more old man!" rasped the Enchantress. "Through my unmitigated carelessness the rogue has obtained the Ultimate Book of Spells – my only copy – to enable me to prevent his loathsome endeavours taking shape!"

"Then what is the key to the solution madam?"

"What is this you say Joe the Tramp? The answer is simple get you gone and -

FIND KING DUNMAIL'S GOLDEN CROWN!"

"Of course!"- replied the Tramp," then everything will be put to rights!" "Therefore!" replied Eli, "let me gaze into my Magic Mirror – the all-seeing picture upon the wall!"

Joe the Tramp looked over her shoulder – to see as Mad Eliza could see! The Mirror darkened as one passes through clouds high above the ground! The all-seeing sight of the Magic Mirror dived through a break in their billowing shapes – and there below a whole army of the Boggart Brood was flowing over the countryside like multitudes of insects would – and the Tramp held his breath knowing what was to come! And there below - the picture moved on – and came upon a great rock rearing upwards into the sky!

"Ah!" growled the Enchantress. "Know you of this Joe the Tramp?"

"Aye Madam!" replied Joe. "It is the home of Millican the Hermit of Castle Rock – the spot reputed to be where the remnants of King Dunmail's men made their last stand!"

"And that be many, many years ago!"

"Verily it be so madam!" replied the Tramp, "- but now Dunmail's lands are once again in dire peril of being turned into a wasteland – and the fight to prevent this will begin where – many years ago - the remains of his army made their final protest!"

"And the King?" asked the Enchantress

"His body was never found – and nor was his Royal Crown of Gold!"

"Ah! Say no more old man - for I hear it was a magical thing! No wonder that High Hat – the Devil Himself - is determined to get his hands on it – therefore we must now find the crown before he does!

"Many agree with you my lady – but the fact is no one knows where to look. It is possible that even at this very moment the Prince of all Evil has –

THE GOLDEN CROWN IN HIS KEEPING!"

When Joe returned along the muddy track by Brothers Water thinking about what the Enchantress had mentioned - how High Hat might have the Golden Crown already in his keeping - plus the enigmatic revelation of the puzzle stated by Lendal. All these would make the task of finding the Golden Crown more baffling than ever.

TEN

The Dancing Pied Piper!

Mr Bill Blenkinsop the owner of a general store in Glenridding looked out from his window – and called to his daughter who was tidying her bedroom.

"Come here Amie! What's happening over the road here?"

Amie hurried from the back.

"Dad whatever's going on?" said Amie.

A host of police vehicles were parked along the main road – and dozens of policemen were hammering on the doors of 'The Glenridding Hotel.' While above - many frightened residents could be seen looking out of the Hotel's opened bedroom windows making frantic efforts to catch someone's attention.

"Whatever is it dad!"

"Nay lass I'm lost for words! Come on! Get your coat on – and we'll have a look!"

They dashed down to the pavement below but by this time the street – was brimming with masses of villagers! While within the hotel Joe the Tramp and Barny and Walter were trying to discover if Peter Pepperson had been found.

"What's happening?" they heard someone say.

With Walter leading the way they encountered a further struggling mass of folk trying to leave the Hotel with their entire burden of luggage.

"I wouldn't go that way!" said an old lady pointing towards a flight of stairs," the police are having a heck of a time with the mob up there!"

"Come on my young friends!" yelled the Tramp, "– I think I can hear Peter's voice!"

They staggered up to the top floor and into the arms of a police lady – and enquired about Peter Pepperson.

"Peter Pepperson? I'm afraid he isn't here – is he a friend of yours?"

"But we've heard his voice!" said Joe. "May we look for him?"

"I'm sorry sir!" announced the Police Constable. "It's chaos up in the roof!"

"May we ask why?" continued the Tramp.

"Well I shouldn't rightly tell you sir – but evidently there's been a lot of strange little men been sleeping up there. Lots of hammocks and things there is! And the mess is absolutely deplorable!"

"Would it be possible for you to give us some further information?"

"Sorry sir," replied the lady Police Officer. "But what I could say - there have been whispers about tins and tins of gold paint!"

They left the hotel in a confused state of mind – and made their way to where Napoleon was bedded down in a disused stable and sat down on one of the many bales of straw scattered around the place.

"This doesn't make sense!" retorted Barny. "Why should they be living in the roof of the hotel?"

"Well it is possible "The Glenridding Hotel is part of the whole business!"

"Come on Joe!" said Barny, "- what business?"

"Obviously," explained the Tramp, "the fact that gold paint was found must mean something!"

"That doesn't explain why Peter Pepperson was kidnapped?"

"Or where they've taken him!"

"Very true Barny!" replied the Tramp.

"Mind you!" mused Barny, "Peter really is knowledgeable about the area around here!"

"His knowledge of Ulfswater?" replied Joe – who then stopped to think.

The three friends realised the significance of what had been stated and paused –

"High Hat requires some local knowledge!" – all shouted. "That narrows things down!" and leaped into the air and cheered! For the moment the excitement overruled every other thought – until Joe went quiet – thinking about the torment of Peter's wife!

Barny and Walter watched Joe the Tramp walk away towards the road leading up to the houses overlooking Glenridding where Peter lived with his wife Sarah. There was nothing to do but stand and stare at the sorry sight of him reluctantly climbing the steep road to where Sarah – Peter's wife - would be waiting for her husband.

"Come on Barny – there's nothing we do at the moment except find Sarah's husband!"

Barny thrust his hands into his pockets – appearing to be quite bewildered.

"Look!" he said, "the thing is – where could they have taken Peter?"

"Under Place Fell – the spot we escaped from?"

"No Walter – too obvious!"

"What then?"

"First of all they could have got him away by Lake Steamer/"

"Definitely not!" replied Walter. "It was getting late and no steamers would be sailing at that hour!"

"By motor boat?"

"Barny! "snapped Walter, "Are they allowed on Ulfswater?"

"Then the obvious solution could be by one of those Golden Vans!"

"True Barny – and one of those would be around – seeing that the raid on the hotel must have been planned in advance!"

"Now where would they take him?" asked Barny." What about Beacon Edge?"

"A little too far I would think!" replied Walter

"Well it's rumoured that Askham Hall is completely deserted!"

"What a cunning ploy!" muttered Walter. "I bet 'you know who' is bluffing!"

However they decided to await the return of the Tramp – not knowing what his state of mind would be having visited Sarah – but they need not have been concerned.

"Sarah is hopeful and sure they'll be reunited!," said the Tramp, "– I agree with your logical assumption – but beware of High Hat - his cunning knows no bounds!"

Several hours later the Green Caravan was on its way heading northwards towards the serene village of Askham – passing through - the extremely silent village of Pooley Bridge.

DRUM! DRUM! DRUMMITY! DRUM!

On they travelled with Napoleon sniffing and snorting the air around them!

"Whatever is the matter with Napoleon!" asked Barny.

"That's a good question my young friend!" relied Joe, "but when uncertain – keep watch and wait!"

The outskirts of Askham were seen just ahead.

DRUM! DRUM! DRUMMITY! DRUM!

"I feel that eyes are upon us!" said the Tramp.

"Me too!" replied Walter.

"And so do I!" agreed Barny. "Huge staring wide-eyed ones!"

"Napoleon seems uneasy!" murmured the Tramp "yet I still feel we've been wrong footed!

"Maybe," replied Walter, "- but this could be one of High Hat's scheming tricks."

However Napoleon settled down and they entered the peaceful village of Askham where in the distance a brass band could be heard playing – and the further along the village street they proceeded the shouts and chatter of adult became louder. Shortly two stone columns were seen on either side of an entrance!"

"The gates of Askham Hall!" exclaimed Walter.

The Tramp hesitated and swung the Green Caravan around to pass silently by the grounds of the Country House - then he sought out a different spot to park Napoleon and the Green Caravan – and this was directly outside 'The Inn of the Red Boar'!

"Now my boys!" said the Tramp, "leave me here with Napoleon to nibble the grass. But from now on remember we are separated. Therefore return to this spot where I've parked the Caravan!

Barny and Walter turned and walked nonchalantly through the gateway of Askham Hall and into the crowds of people chattering upon the vast stately lawns

But whom should they see some way ahead - gossiping within a group of guests but –

GERTRUDE PRIMM AND EDUARDO PLONKS!

But all was not lost! Barny and Walter came upon several friends from Beacon Edge – and were soon gossiping among a circle of friends – therefore what had been expected – being all alone and meeting no one they were acquainted with – never happened.

However the two friends kept a wary eye upon Gertrude and Eduardo –noticing how easily and somewhat familiarly they circulated around the groups of laughing and chattering groups of people.

Once again the festive feeling remained constant - and when the band began to play once again the cheerful mood increased and over the loudspeaker system they heard –

*"MAY IT PLEASE OUR HONOURED GUESTS -
HERE COMES - THE PIED PIPER HIMSELF!"*

A line of young children stormed out through the main entrance of Askham Hall and soon followed by – lots of people applauding.

"Ladies and gentlemen – here is -

THE PIED PIPER"

A very tall gentleman with ginger hair and bright blue eyes and dressed in a multi-coloured suit skipped into the middle of the lawn – and host of children came from within the crowd – and the Pied Piper went skipping and dancing ahead of a joyous line of children – all keeping in time with the shrill sounds of the Piper's notes. Round and about

*"♫ ♪ ♪ ♫ ♫ ♪ ♪ ♪ ♫ ♪ ♫
♫ ♫ ♪ ♪ "*

skipped the red and black costumed Piper. How the crowd clapped shouted. On and on they applauded until finally the Pied Piper led his line of children back through the main entrance and into the Hall.

Once again came more news of festivities –

"LADIES AND GENTLEMEN
– HERE IS AN ABSOLUTE TREASURE -
THE VILLAGE TROOP OF GUIDES AND SCOUTS
WILL NOW PERFORM
THE ANCIENT FLAMBOROUGH SWORD DANCE!"

A tremendous sound of cheering came from every area of the Hall's stately lawns!

CLAP! CLAP! CLAP! CLAP! CLAP! CLAP!

From various speakers around the ground came a musical accompaniment.

And how the crowd enjoyed it – but it was then the two crooks – Gertrude Primm and Eduardo Plonks made their move. Silently and quite unobtrusively they made their way from the lawn and through the entrance into the Hall.

"Now what do we do?" asked Walter.

"Let's see what they're up to – it is my belief something is afoot!"

Chatting confidently the two friends entered the high pillared hallway – and were offered the customary glass of champagne when they crossed the threshold. Drinks in their hands they looked about them – but the two crooks had vanished from view.

Suddenly the Pied Piper appeared!

"Erm! Excuse me sir!" – would you be wanting the lady and gentleman who were just ahead of you? If so I would advise to follow me down into the kitchens below!"

The two friends looked in the direction the Pied Piper had indicated.

Barny and Walter looked surprised then shrugged their shoulders and followed the Piper. He led them through a rather modest entrance and onwards. Shortly they looked upon a rather grim looking doorway followed by a flight of murky steps descending – as it were – into the unknown.

The Pied Piper beckoned them to follow him. Cautiously Barny and Walter stepped downwards into the underworld of Askham Hall and came upon an ancient fireplace within a dimly lighted unused kitchen.

"Gad!" said Barny, "– can I smell soot!"

Walter stepped onwards.

"Mind where you put your feet Walter!" laughed Barny.

The unknown Pied Piper pointed to a set of two footprints leading beyond into the darkness.

Barny hesitated and turned towards the mysterious stranger.

"But this tunnel will lead us far beyond the Hall!

"Exactly!" grunted the Pied Piper. "We've often suspected Askham Hall had its secrets!"

The way ahead was narrow and dark. Their only bearing was a dim patch of daylight hovering ahead in the blackness. Feeling their way with their finger tips touching the passage walls they reached a stout wooden door. The Pied Piper put a finger to his lips and all became silent.

"This will be one of the cellars below The Red Boar Inn!" he whispered and gently pushed the door open. Cautiously they entered a brick lined room where they discovered a wooden stairway leading upwards. Cautiously hearing the sounds of many voices they began to climb upwards.

Not very far from where this was taking place a certain person had an intense glare of light upon him – even when he closed his eyes the light could still be seen. The questions kept coming like waves storming battered beaches. His head ached, sickness invaded his thinking – and above all the loneliness and helplessness that would overcome a lesser man made him more determined to tell them nothing – even though the answers were to him – so simple!

"We'll leave you for the present – but we'll be back – and begin again!"

Something within him made him more determined than ever and Peter ignored his fears.

There he sat in a wheelchair - his wrists and ankles secured by leather straps. When they returned - as they had always returned during the last day or so - it would be as before - the same sharp rasping saw-like voice and the never forgotten sniggering tone! Although blinded by the light the person's Hat seemed too high and the eyes beneath the Hat were cold, sly and ever sinister!

Peter Pepperson was no fool and the one behind the light must be the person Joe the Tramp constantly conjured up – High Hat the Prince of all Evil.

At first this seemed unimportant! But Peter still realised he was still imprisoned – and far from anywhere one would look to find him! He strained at his bonds and he tried to rise from the wheelchair – but it was secured to a hook in a cold stone wall! Time wore on and it became darker! Then he heard –

FOOTSTEPS AND HESITENT WHISPERING!

Footsteps approaching! Footsteps stopping! Someone rattling the iron door of the chamber

"Peter! Peter!"

Peter Pepperson slumped forward –

The iron door opened – and there stood Barny and Walter who looking around them find the Pied Piper had gone!

Peter Pepperson remembered little more – except being propelled speedily across a well-manicured lawn crowded with astonished guests. Later he remembered the snort of a horse and the rattle of harness – and above all the blaring music of brass band!

After a short period of unconsciousness he surfaced lying in a hospital bed surrounded by the Tramp (holding Dusty by a lead) plus Barny and Walter.

"Whatever did they want?" asked Barny

"They're very worried my friend," replied Peter, "from what I could gather they're all very confused regarding Dunmail's golden crown!"

"Yes! I can imagine that Peter," replied Walter, "that will be their end game!"

"No! Not really!" said Peter," from what I could figure out – it's not so much the actual crown itself – but the fact it's made of pure gold!"

"What!" replied Barny, "that really sounds twisted?"

"Not at all!" corrected Joe, "The purity of the golden crown – compared with the fraud began by High Hat upsets the magical situation! And that is not all –

A KING WITHOUT HIS CROWN IS NO KING AT ALL!

For that moment there was complete silence – as they strove to digest the Tramp's scholarly comments!

*****

On the following day - because the present situation was undecided and Walter had gone to apply for a temporary post on a Lake Steamer Joe decided to visit Peter Pepperson. Barny on that very morning decided to go fell walking.

It was such a pleasant afternoon and ahead he observed a suitable spot to eat his sandwiches and take a swig of coffee from his flask. Behind him was the long ridge of Hartsop. However he sat back and relaxed and was just about to take his second bite of his third sandwich (red onion with duck pâté) when he heard sounds of drummimg

Barny – at first – failed to hear anything whatsoever. Then being quite absent minded he looked behind to where the ridge above stared down upon him and

observed a hoard of shouting boggarts, jumping and romping, shrieking and rushing along the slope towards him. Barny swallowed the remaining morsel of his red onion and duck pate sandwich and grabbed his kit and was off like a shot towards the rocky track leading to Fairfield Fell's summit. Behind him came a continuous stream of enraged Boggarts screaming their hatred as Barny stumbled up the steeply rising rocky staircase!

On and on he stumbled! Clawing at each and every rock that blocked his escape. Up and up he darted – dodging the rocks and stones launched at him by the pursuing Brood. He fell and fell again and again – but never allowing the Boggart Brood to seize his ankles! Then a sudden bank of freezing cloud enveloped them and he stumbled once again – and waited for the inevitable of being seized by the dastardly Brood! But it never came. The screams of the Hoard of Boggarts declined – then ceased and he was saved!

The tumbling clouds had thickened and concealed the young man clawing and bleeding in his attempt to reach the top of the track. Upwards and onwards he kept climbing - putting as much distance as possible between himself and the angry Brood.

The clouds eventually cleared and there he crouched looking down from the summit upon Grisedale Tarn where he rested awhile gazing at the scene below!

WHAM!

- two great paws slammed down on each shoulder. Barny turned to look into the stare of a wide glassy-eyed Boggart! Instinctively the young man rammed an elbow somewhere behind him and the Boggart toppled backwards into the arms of another scoundrel. Barny screamed in fear and gained his feet – then slipped and toppled into space and over and over he turned - and miraculously landed on his feet! The sloping scree gave way and down he slid and began to scree-run lifting his feet one foot at a time as if performing a dance then –

BANG!

- the young man knew no more!

He awoke staring at the moon – and how his head ached! A trickle of blood poured down his neck soaking his shirt – its sickly smell filling his nostrils. A hand reached down to pat his shoulder. A gentle hand – one full of concern – the hand of Elfinnus the leader of a tribe of Mountain Guides.

Other figures came into vision – people came around him – lifted him and propelled him shoulder high for many moments as the large silvery moon glared wide eyed down upon them.

Presently journey's end was reached and he was tenderly lowered feet first into cooling water.

"Where am I?" he asked.

"We are approaching the time of great magic and you are standing in the shallows of what humans would call – Grisdale Tarn!" said Elfinnus – and there were grunts of agreement from all about him.

"Sit you down in the waters! "said another, "- and we will bath your head within them!"

Very gently his aching and bleeding body was lowered – and with their cupped hands they scooped up the living waters of the Tarn and poured them over him.

At once he felt at ease and instantly went to sleep where he floated in an exhilarated state of mind - and from on high the large sun beamed down over the countryside where below the young man could hear -

THE TRAMPING OF IRON CLAD WARRIORS!

Barny dived into unconsciousness once again - into the depths of a deep sleep – only to wake once again looking over the Tarn! Somewhere beyond standing alone was a mighty mountain whose top dominated lands in every direction.

Slowly and – above all feeling much more like his old self – Barny found himself stretched out on the banks of the Tarn. Elfinnus was several yards away chatting with the other Mountain Guides. Barny stirred and endeavoured to stand upright. Elfinnus and several others immediately rushed to him and taking the utmost care – steadied him.

"We were so very afraid you were mortally injured and perhaps would fail to recover!"

Barny grunted and put his arm around Elfinnus's shoulder.

"It is not everyone who would recover from a fall from one of the highest and steepest fells around here!"

"Aye! But I had a wonderful dream Elfinnus" and Barny related his visions!

"I heard the Tramp of Armed Men!"

"But that has not happened young man!" assured Elfinnus. "We were standing here and would have seen any procession for ourselves!"

Barny shook his head trying to make sense of his experience.

Elfinnus became insistent -

"Some remnants of Dunmail's army in their confusion may have retreated upwards to the Tarn from the scene of the battle - and that is maybe how the story about Grisedale Tarn began – but the bulk of Dunmail's army would have retreated directly to the north – towards: Castle Crag!

ELEVEN

The Fugitive

When Peter Pepperson stated High Hat was extremely concerned - this was no idle observation. The Prince of all Evil was most aware the one who possessed Dunmail's Crown - especially if it was made of Pure Gold - would be the victor. At this time - the end of October - was yet to come and with it the beginning of the Celtic festival of Samhain. King Dunmail - even though an apparition- was a Celt - and would be aware of this! A time of –

DEEP MAGIC!

- when anything could happen! Because of this High Hat was worried!

"Even though we have Eliza's Book of Spells and full of the world's most magical incantations we must act quickly Frondwagger! Think of the international scandal – should our plans go wrong and we're discovered and the Chinese discover our real intentions!"

Even Frondwagger his Chief Boggart could not think of an answer to the problem.

"Therefore in some way we must destroy the crown's magic thus ensuring our success!"

"Rubbish Frondwagger – we have the Golden Crown thanks to the Enchantress's unique book of spells – but we must keep it for ourselves - and therefore its magic will be ours - and therefore Frondwagger?"

"Its magic," replied the Head Boggart "will make Cumbria ours for evermore!

"Then we will have all the county's mining rights in the palm of our hands!"

"But Master," replied the Chief Boggart, "we must make sure no one knows our secret."

"Just so Frondwagger!" replied High Hat, "let me search The Enchantress's Supreme Book Of Incantations to guarantee our secret – and then we shall see who wins!"

*****

But other things were also occurring! The Tramp and many others knew that time was short - and none more so than Millican.

The Hermit of Castle Rock was sitting by his campfire that very evening when the dark clouds from all points of the compass seemed to swallow up the whole of the darkened sky.

"FLASH! FLIP! FLAP! FLASH! FLASH!"

Millican sat back and looked towards the –

"ZIG! ZAG! ZIG! ZAG! ZIGGING!

- flashes of lightning way towards the east. Again came the flashes of light – bouncing along the tops of the fells all around the heights of Castle Rock. Millican reached forward and quite unhurriedly poured more tea into his large tin mug. He'd seen this happening before

– but had he realised it was the beginning of the Celtic Year – and being a most learned man he should have taken things more seriously.

Once again he leaned back against the rock-face and began to consume his mug brimming with sweetened tea! Once again the flashes of lightning hopped from peak to peak – from ridge to ridge – flipping and zipping through the canopies of forest trees and looked beyond the circle of light!

"CRACKLE!"

Millican reached for his clay pipe and calmly filled it with tobacco but beyond the firelight the bushes had moved!

"CREAK! CRACKLE! CREAK!"

- the Hermit of Castle Rock reached for his handy club – backed slowly towards his cave in the cliff and waited – when wide-eyed fiends came out of the darkness!

Creeping over to the camp-fire's flames an odious group of wild-eyed Boggarts skulked forward! Millican swung his club and a melee of fists – legs and boots hammered Millican to the ground – and there he lay looking upwards into their ugly wide yellow glowing eyes, the mouths oozing with spittle!

But out beyond the circle of light Millican heard the clash of steel on steel – the growl of angry men – and sound pounding of feet on the rocks around the crag were shouts of anger! Belows of fear!

Millican shrank back against the wall of rock – trying to make sense of the moving shadows before him!

The encounter was soon over and shadowy forms of the Boggart Brood went rushing off into the darkness. In the distance came a shrill blast of sound – a staccato of notes of several of the Carnyx:

THE CELTIC WAR
TRUMPET!

- flowing harshly over the night air – and into the firelight came groups of warriors of old!

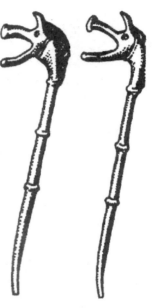

WEARING HEAD PIECES
OF STEEL!
AND COATS OF MAIL!
THEIR MANY BEARED
FACES OLD AND YOUNG!

Millican was helped to his feet – and gently led beyond the firelight – through line upon line of shield bearing warriors – waiting – rank upon rank with anger upon every face

But their gaze was suddenly focussed in the distance! Far ahead and below to where the three limbed lake of Ulfswater glimmered. Steel head pieces turned and steely eyes peered ahead and the chatter of Celtic began to heighten. Below - a crowd lighted torches spread out evenly along the various roads and tracks heading towards Castle Rock. The Warrior's chatter lessened and every man immediately stood to arms – silently, unwaveringly and with pounding hearts.

Millican gulped at the sight below where the infamous Brood were sneaking through consuming twilight. Someone manoeuvred him into a quiet corner against the cliff – and everyone waited in silence.

"DRUM! DRUM! DRUMMITY! DRUM!"

The Boggarts to come to a halt on the road below Castle Rock! The warriors stood to arms and a loud cheer exploded and every warrior's gaze looked upwards to the summit behind them where the King Dunmail himself was standing and lifting their axes bellowed as one – roar after roar!

Millican gave a knowing smile and whispered -

"This indeed is Samhain when the dead stand side by side with the living – but where is the crown?" he asked himself, "- for a king without his crown is no king at all – and therefore his warriors will become dispirited and his cause to retake his country is -

"DOOMED!"

Just as Millican the Hermit decided to slip away as silently as he may – it began to rain. Moving slowly he made his way towards where the rocky track sloped downwards to the road below. Time was short and the people of Ulfswater must be warned and he was the only person at that time aware of the looming disaster!

The rain became a downpour!

Millican hobbled down the twisted track in the dark and set off down the road to Ulfswater Traffic – with their headlights shining – shot by him - soaking him with their spray! On and on he staggered through the night. Nevertheless hours later he walked gamely onward until Millican tripped and lay exhausted by the roadside. Later a driver found his crumpled form and stopped,

An hour later he was carried into the shelter of The Glenridding Hotel where worried staff helped Millican into the nearest seat. However someone contacted Peter

Pepperson and shortly he and Joe the Tramp rushed into the hotel lounge – knowing full well that something important had made the Hermit flee his home on Castle Rock!

"Millican has managed to inform me!" whispered the Tramp. "Dunmail's warriors are ready to a man – "

"But?" retorted Peter Pepperson.

"Aye my friend! But is the word – for if High Hat and his mob of Boggarts attack Castle Rock – that will be the end of it!"

"And God help Ulfswater!"

"Not only that friend Peter," said Joe, "– but most of future Lakeland!"

Then the matter took shape. And the folk of Glenridding and Patterdale rushed off in all directions to inform Ulfswater folk and the importance of their help.

"But when all return - then what?"

"Remember the things of great meaning and of substance," said the Tramp, " – found in Tomes of Wisdom!"

Peter Pepperson laughed – for a well read person was he!

"Friend Joe!"he murmured," there are a myriad explanations in many, many volumes throughout the whole world!

"Maybe friend Peter but what is more important -

'FATE HAS PLACED THREE MEANINGS IN OUR LAPS!"

Peter Pepperson roared with laughter – then sat down to reflect upon what the Tramp had disclosed – and said with a touch of irony in his tone –

"Tell me about these things that Fate has specified!"

The Tramp seemed to conjure up all his being and announced -

"The three things to reflect upon friend Peter are what we already know –

"One - A king is not a king without his crown!"

"Two - Uneasy is the head that wears the crown!"

"Three - Kings and things!"

"So what!" laughed Peter Pepperson.

"And therefore friend Peter which is the most important revelation?"

"You're clutching at straws in the wind Joe – you select one!"

"The first two are what we know," replied the Tramp, "– but what about the last statement?"

"Kings and things?" replied Peter Pepperson. "But why?"

"Kings and things? Because it is my opinion there are more than one king who are concerned my friend!"

"And more golden Crowns as well!" Peter Pepperson laughed sarcastically.

"Not so friend Peter" responded the Tramp.

- BUT THERE ARE TWO KINGS!
KING DUNMAIL AND KING ULF!

- it is also my contention King Dunmail's Crown and King Ulf's crown – are but one of the same crown!'

Throughout the remainder of the day and eventually through the following night the folk of Ulfswater assembled about Glenridding and Patterdale. Shortly the Tramp gathered the leaders together in the main lounge of The Glenridding Hotel.

"We are gathered here to save Ulfswater and most likely a kingdom – a kingdom once lost – and if we succeed and an ancient kingdom regained! Our task is to seize the Golden Crown and put it on the head of King Dunmail – for without it – no matter how he and his warriors make every effort – they will lose the last battle and God help us all if that –comes to pass!'

"This is the procedure," continued the Tramp, "from here we must cross the Lake and reach the far shore and somehow enter the Wall of Light! When we have the crown and God knows how – Elfinnus will seize it and together with our Retriever friend – for in an emergency she will be faster - and deliver it to the Mountain Guides waiting in the boats with the rest of his Guides!"

The assembled leaders sitting comfortably in The Glenridding Hotel almost held their breaths awaiting the rest of the plan.

"Once the Guides – and our friend Dusty are in the boats and have reached Glenridding on the far shore – then the race over the mountains will begin and all being well deliver the crown to King Dunmail's beleaguered forces!"

"One may say this is a leap in the dark – but this would seem to be our only option – now first of all - we must cross the Lake!"

They waited until it began to get dark – when the last rays of the sun went below the fell tops - then in two columns the folk of Ulfswater walked silently along the shore of Ulfswater to where many friends would use their sailing boats to ship the folk of Ulfswater to the far bank beneath Place Fell the home of –

THE MOUNTAIN KING!

In this way their attack would be quite unsuspected and therefore come as a complete surprise.

It was a moonless night when the small armada sped silently across the Lake and the landing of the Ulfswater patriots was quite uneventful. Once the crafts had hit the shallows those aboard waded swiftly through the waters and landed without a sound. Leaders of the throng soon emerged and the advance along the track – considering the lack of moonlight –happened relatively quickly.

It was the Troll called Grieg who directed the final approach to the crag where the "Entrance of Light" was to be found – and there explained to the gathered crowd what they should expect. Grieg with Barny moved forward within a smaller group to where a blazing light from somewhere above.

There - the Troll went through the magical entry routine – and wall within the crag face opened with a sound no louder than a whisper.

The larger groups moved – one by one – and tip-toed behind the leading faction into the jaws of light where they – within the first cavern met an atmosphere of all-embracing silence!

"Stand back!" ordered Grieg, "and be prepared for the worst!"

The entire group of Patriots remained vigilant – but nothing happened. Once again they lingered like tigers ready to pounce – but once again nothing moved or was heard.

Barny and Walter without a second thought stepped forward into the darkness beyond.

*****

A fleet of Golden Vans were speeding towards Ulfswater where many wooden cases were stacked ready to picked up for shipment abroad at the port of Whitehaven. One of these drivers was Eduardo Plonks posing as a chauffeur at Rose Castle - the Palace of the Bishop of Carlisle. When he arrived by the shores of the Lake many of the cases had been taken away by other vans.

The remaining crate was pushed aboard with the help of a willing bystander. Unfortunately Eduardo Plonks hit one of the stones walls on the way down the narrow road leading to Ambleside - dislodging the crate which shot out of the rear doors to burst open scattering the hidden golden ingot far and wide.

Eduardo Plonks panicked knowing the ingots would soon arouse suspicions ran for his life knowing he would soon be a fugitive fleeing from justice and so it was to be. A certain person with bright ginger hair and brilliant blue eyes – a person of middle rank in the Police - was shortly to be hot on his trail.

But Eduardo Plonk's only concern at that moment was to head for Whitehaven where other vans would be unloading the false ingots ready for shipment. It was beginning to rain and it was miserable Eduardo who began looking for shelter. The chug, chug of an ancient motor cycle was heard in the distance which eventually drew alongside of him.

"Want a lift?" asked a bearded old timer!

Eduardo grasped the opportunity and was soon chugging away into the vastness beyond. Eventually they reached the outskirts of Keswick and the Old Timer shook his passenger by the hand and chugged away along the main street. Eduardo Plonks was not unduly perturbed because he had friends here and soon sought them out in one of the many established hotels within the town.

Alfred Sparks the under manager greeted Eduardo as long lost friend who escorted him to a small room on the topmost floor of the hotel. Here Eduardo had an eagle's view of everything that happened on the street below.

Back in Ambleside Alfred Temple alias 'The Pied Piper" - an undercover policeman attached to the Special Branch - was suspicious. The ingots had been moved to the local Police Station where it was discovered the gold paint had been scrubbed away revealing the lead beneath. This came as no surprise - the fraudulent plot to deceive foreign buyers had been known for some time – but how they were to be distributed was unknown.

It was assumed Plonks had disappeared in the direction of Keswick and the local police had been informed. In due course searches were carried out in localities within the town where known crooks conducted their criminal affairs.

Eduardo Plonks high in his eagle's nest on the topmost floor of the hotel happened to see police activity upon the main street below – and incident that caused him to ponder – and even more so when he heard the sound of heavy footsteps coming up the stairs below. Plonk's dived into the nearest wardrobe and pulled the door softly behind him. Someone and shuffled around the bedroom.

"Nothing 'ere guv," said someone.

"No! The boss is just going through the motions," said another, "the Boss has never heard of Eduardo Plonks!"

When the sounds of footsteps had faded away Plonks went down to the restaurant below and sat at a table where he had a good view of all who entered the room. Presently an individual arrived who began looking around the dining room - a tall gentleman with ginger hair and penetrating bright blue eyes – Eduardo Plonks ducked behind a menu page knowing they had met once before at a garden party at Askham Hall.

TWELVE

The Plot That Nearly Failed!

They stepped forward into the Chamber of Light - a huge opening - as though one were entering the belly of a whale – where hooped ridges extended ahead one after another into the unknown.

Way ahead of the Tramp was Dusty straining get ahead on a longish lead. Further ahead was the small army of Ulfswater patriots treading ever onwards towards The Hall of the Mountain King - where the Crown of Gold existed – the true crown – the lost crown of Cumbria.

Finally they reached the final chamber where high marble pillars were set at regular intervals around the walls – where before them - upon a gleaming lofty marble throne sat Ulf the Mountain King who on this occasion appeared more dignified.

"This is not the King we saw before!" whispered Barny to Walter.

"Oh yes it is!" shouted King Ulf, "I've got ears you know – and I've been told to behave like a proper king – be a bit refined and sort of posh!"

The Tramp by this time had pushed his way through the crowd of Patriots.

"Greetings your Majesty," said the Tramp who bowed very low, "may I offer you my thanks for this audience?"

"Who is this twit?" asked King Ulf," he's not supposed to be here – he's not on my list!"

It was then the Tramp noticed his Majesty was not wearing his crown!

"More problems my friends!" he muttered. "We must treat this crisis with the utmost care!"

"Too true!" whispered Walter. But Dusty had sensed something was wrong and began to whimper. Folk nearby then began to whisper – and someone noticed the absence of the crown upon the head of King Ulf. People began to turn and point their fingers.

"Look!" cried someone. "He's not wearing the crown."

"Oh my Lord!" cried the Tramp.

But more and more Patriots began mutter – and very soon the whole assembly began to protest.

"High there your majesty! Where's your crown?"

The chatter increased and more and more people began ask the same question:

"WHERE'S YOUR CROWN?"

Joe ran forward and began to urge everyone to calm down – but he went unheard and the uproar increased.

King Ulf leaped to his feet and appealed for silence.

The clamour ceased and everyone listened. King Ulf pondered for a and a crafty gleam came into his eyes when exclaimed:

"Willie the Chamberlain has the Crown – and he's going to clean it!"

In an instant roars of laughter pervaded the Hall – even the Tramp began sway with laughter.

"Well where is Willie?" shouted many.

"Come on Ulf," bellowed another. "Come on! Come clean!"

Ulf began to tremble most fearfully.

"It could be in my royal apartments – but you'll have to go through all the procedures!"

"And what are they?" laughed the crowd.

Barny stepped forward and announced, "– first of all we have to pass through The Portal of a Thousand and One Knocks!"

The crowed on hearing this were speechless.

"Then comes The Steps of Numbers!" continued Barny

The crowd listened most attentively.

"And then you'll be stopped by His Majesty's Body Guards – The Royal Candle Bearers!"

"Is that the lot?" shouted the Patriots.

"That's enough!" replied Walter, "just wait and see!"

King Ulf went ahead and everyone followed - and shortly they reached a stout oak door studied with precious twinkling stones – which was partly open.

"The Portal of a Thousand and One Knocks, "replied King Ulf, "– is open!"

"Therefore?" asked the Barny.

"It means young fella – there'll be no snags ahead!"

"Not even The Steps of Numbers?" asked the Tramp.

"No mate – not even them!"

"What about your bodyguards," enquired Walter, "– the Royal Candle Bearers?"

"Don't worry pal," replied King Ulf. "I'll soon settle them!"

Just ahead were the Royal Candle Bearers all standing dutifully in line with bowed heads.

"I told you," said King Ulf, "I've got a good grip on this lot!"

Finally the entered his Majesty's Royal Chamber – and there upon King Ulf's throne someone was waiting.

"Oh dear!" said King Ulf. "It's Willie the Chamberlain!"

They were dazzled by the curtain of light behind the throne and attempted to see beyond its intense glare – where a dark shape emerged. Behind were more Royal Candle Bearers - the bodyguards of the King

"Foreigners!" bellowed the shrouded person, "– do you think I'm unaware of your visitation? Is it not the Crown of Cumbria you desire? See behind me and there it is for all to see!

The Royal Candle Bearers who were standing behind Willie the Chamberlain – surged forward and positioned themselves before the crowd of Patriots.

"There before you," roared Willie," gasp at the sight of the serene Golden Crown of Cumbria!"

The Patriots gazed in astonishment at the gleaming sight of the lost crown of Cumbria being held high in the air by one of Willie's the - Chamberlain's tallest bodyguards.

Grieg the Troll who had by now become encircled by the surge of the Bodyguards – instantly took his chance and leapt upwards to grasp King Dunmail's crown!

His intention being, to grasp the crown and toss it to Elfinnus one of the Mountain Guides. But Grieg at that moment tripped and fell among the crowd and the Golden Crown was soon within the grasp of Willie the Chamberlain. Everyone wailed in despair and ran for their lives knowing the lost crown of Cumbria could only be taken by King Dunmail himself.

*****

Detective Sergeant Alfred Temple was quite aware the gentleman with the scruffy black hair was hiding – and glanced idly around the dining area. Then after a long pause – walked casually through the door and out onto the pavement – then even more indifferently - walked out of sight. The crook Eduardo Plonks was most concerned and realised he'd been spotted and under suspicion. It was vital for him to be at the docks at Whitehaven because he was the one responsible for the loading of the loot - as it were – onto the Motor Vessel 'Shylock' on route to Amsterdam. Eduardo did as most crooks would do – he attempted to disappear.

He wiped his mouth quite nonchalantly on his napkin and wandered out of the dining room through the toilet area and onto the back lawn – and at a gallop headed for a clump of ornamental shrubs at the end of a rear garden and crouched very low. After satisfying himself all was safe he walked to the nearest bus stop and presently boarded the next bus into the centre of the Keswick.

From there Eduardo Plonks sought out a certain bookshop owned by Ernie Shanks who owned a fast car and after an hour's polite conversation – or so it would seem – Eduardo Plonks was soon speeding towards Whitehaven.

This car soon approached Wythop Woods and there yet a further car pulled out three hundred yards behind him and there it stayed. Eduardo Plonks who was listening to his local radio station hadn't the slightest inkling he was being followed. But there the other car remained – a black dot on his mirror – all the way to the docks at Whitehaven

The black police car purred into the waterfront and sought out the ships ready to sail - then motored up and down the quay surveying all the motor vessels being made ready to depart on the next tide. Many suspicious craft were noted and the police stationed themselves to see but not be seen. However Eduardo Plonks - the crook – knew the plan – the plans to hijack one of the sailing ships crewed by young people and slyly sail away to the Isle of Man where the Organisation had their headquarters.

That night when the crew were granted leave – they went ashore and discover the intricate nightlife of Whitehaven the seaboard town. During the evening in their absence Eduardo and other crooks loaded the false ingots aboard and the sailing ship slipped away on the following tide and sailed for the Isle of Man.

D/S Alfred Temple was happy in the knowledge of having sealed off all escape routes from the harbour and at that very moment all suspect ships were being investigate for hidden contraband. D/S Alfred Temple stretch out in the back of his car and cherished the thought of wrapping up the whole case by the morrow quite unaware the birds had flown.

But circumstances changed dramatically and D/S Alfred Temple together with other anti-smuggling craft were ordered to put to sea. Those who were directing the operation were in a quandary and realised they had been deceived – but nevertheless they were quite mystified about how the irregularity had come about. But quite unknown to them the sailing ship was being safely harboured in the Isle of Man's port of Douglas.

Eduardo Plonks and other crooks left the craft at her moorings and went ashore to sample a variety of the port's nightlife especially the Hilton Night Club where they were asked to dance by stunning young ladies.

Eduardo Plonks surveyed the scene – where his crew of crooks joined the laughing, happy, excited dancers swirling around the dance floor. Eduardo hovered for a few moments before retreating to the bar where he had a certain appointment to keep.

A smartly dressed young gentleman wearing a floppy trilby hat was waiting for him and quickly made some arrangement. Eduardo Plonks followed the stranger from the bar and out onto the street. And down several dingy passageways. Eventually there before them a flight of stairs led downward to where a bright light showed beneath a door. The young man ahead pushed a bell-push and the door slowly opened.

There came an exchange of gruff voices and the door opened wider and a rush of cold air made them stagger backwards. The sound of ship's engines and the smell of the sea were overpowering. They went ahead into a large cellar where gold coloured ingots were being packed away into wooden barrels and stood in lines. A group of seamen were trundling these away on sack barrows and stacked these upon an open quayside. Around them were the open docks where the lights of waterfront glimmered on the heaving surface of the sea. Eduardo Plonks stood watching and waiting expectantly not knowing why he had been escorted to this particular situation – but the young man in the floppy trilby had gone!

Soon after three uniformed policemen came from behind and led him away – now knowing he'd been tricked!

*****

Things happened very quickly. Knowing the plot had failed and they must reorganise. Grieg unlocked the barrier of light – and followed by Elfinnus and the remainder of the Mountain Guides made their escape knowing Willie the Chamberlain and his men would soon be after them. Dusty was the first to reach the open air and the first to reach the waiting boats. Barny and Walter now way behind - reached the shore just in time to jump aboard. The craft cast off - its prow slicing its way through the waters of Ulfswater towards the shores of Glenridding.

The last to leave the Chamber of Light was Joe the Tramp and the crowd of Patriots - who reached the waiting crafts and jumped aboard. By this time the Royal Body Guards were speeding after them.

When the first boat grounded on the far side of the Lake they waited for the Tramp to step ashore and a hasty Council of War was organised on the spot.

"We must somehow persuade King Dunmail to leave Castle Rock and march his warriors here – for this is the place he must reach to claim his Royal Crown!"

The group of Patriots around the Tramp applauded and set off to trek over the fells. Dusty once again took the lead and continued to race ahead with Barny trying to restrain her on a lead. The plan was to take a route along the road below the screes of Sheffield Pike.

"We'll get ahead as quickly as we can," ordered Elfinnus," – then we'll rest up at the old Youth Hostel which is some way ahead of us where our way over the mountain tracks begin!"

Everyone laughed and struggled on.

DRUM! DRUM! DRUMMERTY! DRUM!

"Boggarts!" shouted Barny looking behind them, "– lots of them – are coming towards us from Glenridding!"

Everyone looked back down the road where hoards of the Boggart Brood were heading uphill towards them – but way beyond them standing alone in Glenridding was Joe the Tramp – who realised an old man, would be on encumbrance – and therefore preferred to stay behind.

"This is a race against time!" bellowed Elfinnus. "There'll be no point in resting up! At present they're not gaining on us!"

They huffed and they puffed and stormed onwards– and swung right and up the ridge where the going was steep and rough. Eventually they stopped for a breather at the remains of an old reservoir - and looked back to see the Brood still behind them!

"Not to worry!" laughed Elfinnus. "They find this last pitch just as strenuous to get up here!"

They stormed ahead but once again they looked back and to their horror it was obvious the Brood were gaining on them.

"Follow me!" shouted Elfinnus. "We Mountain Guides know the best route – we'll head for Sticks Pass!"

Much, much later – and thoroughly exhausted – they reached the ridge route - and looked back – and not a Boggart was to be seen!

"If they've taken a different path," laughed Elfinnus – they'll have found it much harder!

Ahead was easier walking with sweeping grassy slopes and they were hard pressed and therefore it took three hours reach the summit of Stybarrow Dodd the first in the series of peaks before their goal of Castle Crag – where ahead they heard the dull roar of people and indistinct class of metal.

"My God!" murmured Elfinnus, "are we too late?"

"How do we get down to Castle Crag?" asked Walter. "From here – the way ahead looks a bit confusing."

Elfinnus and the rest of the Guides knowing the fells as they knew them – smiled.

"Head for the fell beyond us!" replied Elfinnus. "It be called Watson's Dodd and we can follow the ridge down to Castle Rock!"

They stumbled on – and finally the scene below opened at their feet -

- where the Boggart Brood in full battle dress of chainmail – bearing an axe or a sword - were directed by a strange high hatted figure standing upon a high eminence flourishing his wand! Here! There! This way! That way! Up! Down! And about! And where his spell fell - iron clad warriors were falling back!

Standing tall above his shrinking army King Dunmail roared his battle cry when in turn the warriors around him raised their hands in adulation crying –

"THE KING! THE KING!
BRING BACK THE KING OF CUMBRIA!"

On and on roared the beleaguered mass of men –
knowing without the Crown of Cumbria – they were
doomed.

Even without the Crown upon his head - the warriors
around him roared in approval and the course of the
battle changed. The warrior's confidence was renewed
and the ebb and flow of the strife – and the entire
conflict changed! And step by step the hideous Brood of
Boggarts were driven back to the edge of the cliff – and
further.

Many were pitched into the void beyond. The Celts
advanced – shield to shield and drove the remaining
Boggarts down the mountain. The Celtic war trumpet
blared- and the entire army advanced quickly shouting:

"HAIL THE KING! HAIL DUNMAIL!"
-THE LAST KING OF CUMBRIA!"

And the Boggarts who survived could be seen heading
away into the distance and the Prince of all Evil
panicked and stepped down from the high rock and
merged with rest of the Boggart Brood who were now in
full retreat. High Hat was gone and swallowed within
the swarming mass of the Brood heading to the road
below.

It was now quite dark and a full moon showed her
face lighting the fells all around with her own eerie
silvery glow. It was now The Time of the Ancients and
the beginning of the Celtic festival of Samhain – seed

fall and a time when the dead would sit with the living around their camp fires. And this being so Elfinnus and the other Guides although used to being on the verge of Magic all of their lives – waited in hesitant expectations. On the other hand the two young Barny and Walter had no experience of the other world or its illusions and waited to be - as it were - entertained by a theatrical performance.

Eventually - the time of Samhain was now - and when the many campfires began to spread around them – Barny and the living were loath to sit with the spirits of the dead – when drinking horns were being passed around – and the quaffing of ale and the inebriated voices laughed and the jesting began, then they slept!

When they slept. The mysteries about them faded when they reclined into slumber and on waking they immerged sleepy-eyed into a world neither living nor dead. But there was Magic in the air and the campfires were out and Dunmail himself had stood Sentinel that night – and realised the Crown must be found and taken. On his orders the Celtic began mustering themselves into columns for the Long March across the hills to settle with the Devil himself.

Still watching from on high the two young men and Elfinnus with the rest of the Mountain Guides suddenly realised what was happening and were determined somehow to lead the Celtic Warriors safely across the fells and down to Ulfswater where the last crown of Cumbria was to be sought out.

The first few miles were strenuous – treading the upward pitch of the slopes – where the cloud base slipped lower and lower where all were marching onwards into the mist. With the unerring tread of Elfinnus leading the columns through the mysterious fog the summit of Raise appeared and Sticks Pass was somewhere before them. There they rested in the freezing arms of the miasma – then the Celtic War Trumpet sounded – and the race against time began.

DOWN! DOWN! DOWN!
TREAD! TREAD! TREAD!

Into the freeing fog – where icicles were everywhere! Drooping from ears and noses! From shields and shouldered axes –

THE ICICLES DROOPED AND DRIPPED!

Eventually the Youth Hostel building loomed out of the gloom where

TIREDNESS AND SWEAT -

were their constant companions!

DOWN! DOWN! DOWN!

- ever downwards stumbled the avenging Celtic Army – until a bearded old man dressed in a tattered gabardine coat loomed before the first column of warriors – when Barny and Walter streaked ahead to shake Joe the Tramp by the hand.

"By all the Saints! "muttered the Tramp who turned and pointed into the darkness. "Hear the commotion across Ulfswater?"

They listened. From beyond in the direction of Place Fell sounds of mayhem drifted across the waters towards them."

"Is this the end?" shouted Barny.

"Not on your life my friend – what is occurring yonder is the beginning of a full blown insurrection! Willie and his men are in trouble!"

Then the surface of the Lake began to heave and high waves began to shoot onto the road – and finally the surface of the road began to –

SHUDDER! SHUDDER! SHUDDER!

and -

CRACK! CRACK! CRACK!

"This is the turning of the Final Saint friend Walter!" shouted the Tramp.

The Carnyx sounded again and the ten columns of warriors advanced

SHIELD TO SHIELD!

- and through Patterdale towards the neck of Ulfswater – went the relentless tread of the advancing columns –

where the trees around formed a tunnel where hefty boughs began to break and tumble down before them. The marchers stopped! Way behind and beyond Eliza the Enchantress had been peering into her Magic Mirror:

"So Dunmail the King is fighting for his Golden Crown after all – and now the final act of High Hat's miserable saga is to be unveiled and my precious Book of Spells will be soon in my possession once again."

The White Witch turned and taking up her magic wand cursed the name of High Hat the Prince of All Evil:

"SUCKER PLUM! HUM! HUM! HUM! – TURN AGAIN AND RUN! RUN! RUN! – THRICE TIMES NINE TO NINETY-NINE - SOAK THE NIT IN SOURED WINE! NOW! NOW! NOW!"

The earth ceased to move for a moment! The waves upon the Lake slightly quietened –and the avenging Celtic Army charged en masse towards the crag and the Curtain of Light.

At this very moment many of the rebellious Trolls were locked in mortal combat with a whole regiment of Royal Candle Bearers the Body Guards of Willie the Chamberlain. Many Trolls retreated and surged through the Curtain of Light and out onto the open fellside. Once again the Carnyx sounded -

WAAAAAA! WAAAAA!

The first ranks of the Celtic warriors were greeted joyously by King Ulf ahead of the fleeing Trolls – yet the Celtic army marched on through the Curtain of Light and into the void beyond.

DOWN! DOWN! DOWN!

- into the unknown depths marched King Dunmail and his cheering warriors!

SHUDDER! SHUDDER! SHUDDER!

- and into the Pillared Hall of the Mountain King!

Way back in Beacon Edge the final Saint was beginning to turn its back on the world in disgust and the pillars around the Hall seemed to move one way and then the other. The cataclysm was approaching. The Hall of the Mountain King began to topple one by one - bit by bit – this way and that way! Pieces of the ornate ceiling became loose and fell away to land among the ranks of Celtic warriors - who remained steadfast and of a single resolve to take back the Crown of Dunmail the Last King of Cumbria.

CRASH!

The whole roof began to give way – but the spirit of the Celts remained firm in their resolve!

"There's the Crown!" shouted Walter, "– it's hanging on high from one of the chandeliers!"

And so it was! The Lost Crown of Cumbria gleamed and twinkled for all to see!

"We're doomed!" shouted some of the Trolls. "The Hall is beginning to collapse!"

The Golden Crown began to teeter and slip!

"Don't just stand there!" bellowed the Tramp. "Catch the thing!"

But all were rooted to the spot!

A streak of gold shot out of the crowd and in one gigantic leap Dusty the golden retriever snatched the Lost Crown of Cumbria before it smashed to pieces upon the stone floor!

AN OLD STALWART WARRIOR –
SEIZED THE LOST CROWN

- and ran to where King Dunmail was standing and knelt down before his master! Then followed a serene and delicate moment when the Last King of Cumbria took the golden crown within his hand – and in an act of reverence that was almost Holy placed the Lost Crown of Cumbria upon his head!

INSTANTLY ALL THE BELLS IN EVERY CHURCH

- rang joyously throughout Cumbria!

"GOD SAVE KING DUNMAIL"

- shouted everyone!

Saint Botolph's Church in Beacon Edge sounded the loudest for the last of the Five Saints decided not to turn

151

– and now the Lost Crown had been placed upon the head of Dunmail the Last King of Cumbria

'NOW EVERYTHING IS AS IT SHOULD BE!'

THIRTEEN

Did Everyone Live Happily Evermore?

1. Saint Botolph's Church in Beacon Edge sounded the loudest for the last of the Five Saints never turned! Saint Bega's Church in Eskdale Green reverberated – and in Whitehaven all the bells rang out. Eduardo Plonks heard them when being driven in a Prison Van to serve a Long sentence for theft and deception. Weeks later Eduardo received a letter from Gertrude Primm who had flown back to South America.

My Dear Eduardo,

Never forget we have friends everywhere and we will meet again sooner than one would imagine. The moment I have settled myself here in this foreign land, I we'll have you here with me! Our friend High Hat has friends here and everywhere, so do not despair!

Gertrude Primm

2. As for Eliza the Mad Enchantress who had her Book of Spells returned -but not by King Dunmail himself as she had surmised. The occurrence was found in her Witch's Diary -

Quite by chance I was working down in my most secret chamber where the subterranean winds are always howling – I happened to be sorting through my most secret papers when I chanced upon finding my Magic Briefcase! The one I take with me when travelling on my broomstick – and there it was? Lying under a secret address list of all my White Witch associates was my Ultimate Book of Secret Spells! I was so happy I drank a whole bottle of my favourite Elixir!

3 For the moment nothing was discovered below the Four Gravestones upon Castle Rock – yet many years later two skeletons were found showing grave injuries around the eyes sockets! (It is a point of history that King Dunmail's two sons were captured by King Edmund and blinded in an infamous act of barbarism!)

4 As for Lendal the Old Crone of Dalemain – she still lives there and if it is allowed she can still be found in her most secret of her secret Libraries. If you seek out Dusty the Golden Retriever who still lives in Glenridding she may help one to discover its secrets.

5. Cumbria never became an industrial mining centre and the haul of false ingots was revealed to the Government of China and no one was deceived or shamed.

The Intercontinental Airliner lowered its flaps and began a long careful approach to the runway – where below - the supreme Chairman of the Chinese Regime awaited the Prime Minister of Her Majesty's Government.

The massed bands began to play and the ranks of the Chinese Guards came swiftly to attention and the British National Anthem began to play. Her Majesty's Prime Minister having inspected the ranks of the Guard of Honour - he and his entourage were whisked away in shining limousines to a secret location within the city.

Later in the Hall of Warriors hundreds of guests sat down to a sumptuous meal – an occasion whereby no expense was spared. Then followed the speeches whereby the Supreme Chairman thanked the representative of Her Majesty's Government for exposing the plot to deceive his Government and thereby preventing an International humiliation.

6. Later it was said – His Majesty King Ulf the First of the Hall of the Mountain King stated in a personal interview:

"It's a Topsy Turvy world you know – no one knows 'what' is 'what' or 'which is 'which.' It is probable that 'Willie' isn't 'Willie' at all – and 'His Nibs' maybe someone else! 'Willie' may actually be High Hat – or High Hat perhaps could even be 'His Nibs' - not forgetting the bloke with the Roman nose – or could he be the one with the 'pot belly?'

It doesn't matter who they are because the –

DEVIL IS ALWAYS WITH US!
WHOM DO YOU THINK WAS HIGH HAT?"

7. And the Pied Piper? What became of the red haired policeman? Well he found his profession was too tame and returned to what he did in the first place! A professional Circus performer - high over the Ring! The stylish young man on the flying trapeze!